The Source

A Novel by Alastair Anderson

1

She put the drinks down and we watched her go. Her tunic was snug against her body, crisp and white and without a trace of sweat. She stepped quietly across the deck, disappearing into the darkness of the cabin.

"Help yourselves," said Valassis, reaching for a beer from the ice bucket.

We all followed his example. Jongstra smiled as he read the label on the can. "Saigon special."

"I'm out of Carlsberg," said Valassis, snapping the tab.

"It's not bad," I said. "Not a bad beer at all."

Valassis turned to the newcomer, inspecting him for the first time. "What did you say your name was?"

"Carraway. Chris Carraway." He had black hair and pale skin, the kind that burns easily. He must have just arrived in Vietnam.

The four of us drank in silence, listening to the insistent slapping of the river against the bottom of the hull. A continuous flow of sampans buzzed past, for the most part visible only by a skipper's head passing along the gunwale while he stood guiding his vessel with an outboard engine. Valassis' yacht was raised on its keel alongside the quay.

Our host looked around at us as he took a sip of beer. "Who's got something to say?"

Nobody replied. None of us knew each other at all.

I turned to Carraway, because he was so much younger. The rest of us had at least age in common. "You look like you could tell us something we don't know."

He took a swallow of beer and sat back, smiling. "That would be hard."

"Why?"

"It looks like you've all done pretty well for yourselves."

Jongstra smiled. "Valassis has his yacht. What are you assuming for the rest of us?"

"Your Rolex, for starters."

"It could be fake. This is Vietnam."

Carraway shook his head. "I've seen a good few of those to know. What do you do for a living?"

"I'm an accountant."

"And you?" He looked at me.

"A lawyer."

"And you?" Carraway turned to Valassis, who was clearly unimpressed with the directness of the question.

"Company director," he replied at last.

"What about you?" I said.

Carraway shrugged. "Nothing much."

"What are you doing in Vietnam?"

"The same as all of you."

"And how would you know what we're doing?"

Carraway shrugged, looking out over the Mekong. "Just guessing."

Sampans scratched their wakes across a river that was slack and worn-out in the afternoon sun. But the tide had turned and soon it would be back, lifting the yacht out of its isolation and returning it to the motion of the water.

"Well?" said Valassis, scratching the stubble on his chin. "Have none of you got anything to say?" He looked annoyed. It was his yacht. We should come up with something if we wanted to remain his guests.

We looked at each other. Four white men, each of us alone and away from home. Four men with nothing to do but wait.

"Alright," said Carraway. "I'll tell you all a story."

"What's it about?" said Jongstra.

"Something you don't know," he said with a smile.

"You just told us that you couldn't."

"I haven't really succeeded in anything, but it's given me a story."

"Experience is what you get when you get nothing else," said Valassis, pouring his beer into a glass. "Get on with it then. This boat will be sailing with the tide."

"That's all the time I need." Carraway took a sip of beer and sat back against the gunwale. "Let me start when I was in college."

"Is that relevant?"

"Not really. But it's a good place to start."

A beer can clattered as Valassis tossed it into the bin. "I'll tell you something. Life isn't about starting, it's about finishing. You've got an hour."

2

"I started college in the right way. I was sure that I was on the brink of a period of profound self-discovery. Things would fall into place and I would find a centre, and with that the power and the purpose to go out into the world and do things. Extraordinary things." Carraway paused, looking around at us. "It never happened. I felt *it* must be out there, somewhere. But by the time I graduated, I realised that it hadn't even slipped through my fingers. It never existed."

The yacht rocked as a wave slapped heavily against it. A barge chugged past, leaving the surrounding sampans bobbing in its wake.

"How old are you?" said Jongstra.

"Thirty-three, so that was twelve years ago. I left college pretty much as I'd arrived, although with a qualification."

He smiled. "That's a nice word, isn't it? I went in one end full of possibility, and came out the other end qualified."

"Qualified in what?" I asked.

"Law."

"Could be a lot worse."

"But consider why I did it. Simply because it could be useful. Whatever happened, it would keep me from sweeping streets. So I was already resigned, at what should have been a pivotal point in my life, to a simple practicality."

"That's your story?" I said. "You regret becoming a lawyer?"

Carraway shook his head. "I qualified, but I never practised law. I wanted to do something different. Something, anything. As long as it was different."

"So here you are, bumming around South-east Asia."

"That comes later." Carraway picked up his beer and took another sip. "I did various things at first, not really sticking with anything. Following the money, falling out with that and then following it again. After a few years in finance I ended up working in Switzerland. Has anyone here heard of the Bank for International Settlements? It's mainly known by its acronym, the BIS."

Jongstra nodded.

"Do you know what they do?"

"It's some kind of regulatory organisation."

"It's much more than that. Nearly everyone thinks that the world's central banks have the final say in finance. Well, they don't. The BIS does. It's known as the central bankers' bank."

"How did you end up there?" I asked.

He shrugged. "How does anyone end up anywhere? Largely by accident. I could never have imagined working there. They're a bunch of bureaucrats on secondment, so they're as removed from any accountability as you can get." Carraway squinted in the sunlight, the only one of us who wasn't wearing sunglasses. The sun was low in the sky and the awning didn't provide much shade. "It's not surprising that there've been plenty of conspiracy theories that the BIS is a front organisation, set up to control the world. Of course, it doesn't help matters with its culture of secrecy. It's not accountable to any government, only its members."

"And who are they?" I asked.

"All the main central banks. Like the Federal Reserve, the European Central Bank, and the Bank of England."

"And the conspiracy theories? What of those?"

"I wouldn't really know. But everything has a grain of truth, doesn't it? The BIS has had a chequered past. It was founded in the nineteen-thirties, to handle payment of German reparations to the allies. The original board of directors had several senior ranking Nazis, some of whom were convicted at Nuremburg. After the Second World War, it came to light that the bank helped launder assets that the Nazis had stolen from occupied countries. Roosevelt was determined to shut it down, but he died before he could make that happen."

Jongstra put down his beer. "Are you for real? The foremost bank in the world had links to the Nazis?"

"It's a fact. Not well known perhaps, because hardly anyone has heard of the BIS, let alone having any idea of what it does. Its main aim is to ensure the stability of the global banking system. It sets the standards that govern banking capital all over the world." Carraway turned to look as a diesel engine rattled noisily behind him. A barge slipped past, barely afloat beneath its load of timber, the bow wave lapping over its gunwale. "Do any of you know that Switzerland has a port?"

Without looking at us for confirmation, he continued. "Thanks to the Rhine, it does. A town called Basel, where the BIS has its headquarters. It's a quiet and orderly place. A town engaged in discreetly gathering wealth, no questions asked. It wasn't just the BIS that acted as a conduit for Nazi gold, but several of the other banks in Basel as well. That never came out until the nineties, when a security guard was told to shred documents which he turned over to the newspapers instead."

"Where are you going with this?" said Valassis.

Carraway smiled. "I apologise. I'm digressing. The point is that I ended up in Basel, at the Bank for International Settlements. It was just a temporary contract at first, but I kind of liked it and stayed on."

"You're telling us you had a life-changing experience by getting a job at a bureaucracy in Switzerland?"

"It's just the start of my story."

Valassis turned and watched the river for a few moments. It had been as still as a lake, but was starting to ripple with the return of the tide. "I suggest you get on with it. This yacht isn't going to stick around forever."

"I hadn't been there long when the BIS set up a new secretariat, aiming to supervise not only banks, but the entire global financial system. It was just as the financial crisis was starting to break."

"Did it do any good?" I asked.

Carraway shrugged. "Hard to say. The issues were very complex."

"Give it to us in your own words. What exactly was the problem?"

"It's the old idea of a butterfly flapping its wings in China, and causing a hurricane on the opposite side of the earth. Since financial markets were deregulated in the eighties, capital can flow freely around the world and everything has become increasingly interconnected, so much so that a small effect somewhere can be magnified many times in seemingly unrelated areas.

The global financial system has become so huge and complex that it's impossible to know if any imbalances have built up, or what their consequences could be. For some time now, financial markets have been moving more and more wildly, and most concerning, in tandem. So a sudden change in a market or an individual security could be multiplied many times across the world, and there's nowhere to hide because everything has a direct influence on everything else." Carraway paused, taking another sip of beer. "Before I start digressing again, let me get to the point. Has anyone here heard of Joseph Klein?"

Valassis looked up. "What about him?"

"They wanted me to investigate him."

"What for?"

Carraway shrugged. "Let's call it an enquiry."

"What about?"

"Hold on a minute," I said. "Who is Joseph Klein?"

Carraway turned to me. "Klein controls one of the largest and most successful hedge funds in the world."

"And they wanted you to investigate him?"

Carraway nodded.

"Why?"

"Let me put it in context. As I said, the financial crisis was just starting to take hold. A butterfly had flapped its wings. In this case it was house prices in America, which unleashed a financial hurricane around the world.

Property prices had been rising for so long that everyone had come to believe that would always be the case. Forever up, and up, and up, leading people to take on more and more debt, which they could only ever repay if the houses on which they had raised that debt kept on inflating.

Their mortgages were sold on by the banks, packaged and repackaged into increasingly complex financial instruments which were far removed from the original house purchase, but at the same time still dependant on that house continuing to appreciate in value.

But then out of the blue house prices stopped rising. Anyone would have said that was no big deal, because they hadn't dropped. They'd just flattened out. But because debt levels were so high, it was enough to sow the seeds of a collapse."

"Tell us something we don't know," said Valassis, putting down his beer. "Lan!"

We sat in silence until she appeared in the cabin doorway.

"Another round of drinks, and more ice. Plenty more ice."

We watched her collect the ice bucket from the deck at our feet. She moved with perfect poise while we slouched in the heat. She carried the ice bucket downstairs, banging it against each step as if to make a point.

"So you had to investigate Klein," said Valassis, watching Carraway closely. "What did you find?"

Carraway gave a half-smile, watching the cabin entrance where the woman had disappeared. It was pitch-black in the bright afternoon sunlight. "Let me start on the day I was called into my supervisor's office."

3

"It was a February morning in Basel. I arrived at work with my tie cut off, because of the carnival."

"Come again?" said Jongstra.

"Basel has a carnival the week after Mardi Gras. February is invariably grey and cold, but people take the whole thing very seriously, starting festivities well before dawn. As I was walking to work, bands were roaming the streets dressed in jester outfits with huge papier-mâché heads. They were cutting off people's ties, because you're not in the spirit of things if you're wearing one." Carraway paused, looking around at us. "Have any of you been to Basel?"

We shook our heads.

"It's a strange place. Right at the epicentre of Europe, where France and Germany and Switzerland all meet. You'd think that it would be bursting with the energy of a continent, but it's not. The heart of Europe is closed. While Basel seems to come alive with Mardi Gras, it's impossible for outsiders to penetrate. And yet, things happen there. Things with global consequences.

I arrived at work to find that my supervisor wanted to see me. There were three other people in his office, sitting around his desk. He introduced only one of them. The man was smoking, even though it's banned in the bank's offices. His name was Thys. A Belgian.

Having made the introduction, my supervisor left me alone with them. None of the men seemed to notice that my tie was sliced off. The cut was very Swiss. Clean and clinical, with no frayed edges. As I sat down, Thys stood up and walked across to the window.

"Have you heard of Atracor Capital?" he said, looking out.

I nodded.

"What do you know of it?"

"One of the largest hedge funds, run by Joseph Klein."

"And what do you know of him?"

"Not much. In fact, nothing at all."

Thys nodded. "Klein has a well-deserved reputation for secrecy." He took a draw on his cigarette as he looked out at Basel's grey skyline, releasing the smoke to drift in front of the glass. "Klein is one of the world's most successful investors, and yet he was originally an academic. He prefers to be known as Dr Klein. He has PhDs in mathematics and computer science. He was a pioneer in quantitative investing, developing computer programmes to identify anomalies in the market. He was the first to combine multiple processors to analyse massive amounts of data."

Thys paused for a moment, running his fingernail across the window as if he were feeling for a crack in the glass. "Klein's proprietary trading algorithms are a tightly held secret. It's like Coca-Cola guarding the formula for their syrup. His firm is so secretive that its employees are forbidden from telling anyone who they work for. Atracor Capital is set up very much like a front company. Such is Klein's thirst for secrecy, that he's gone to great lengths to ensure that there's nothing of substance connecting him to the firm. But in reality the two of them are one and the same." Thys took another draw on his cigarette. His colleagues sat watching me in silence. "Any questions?" he asked, still with his back to me.

"What's he done wrong?"

"Nothing specifically."

"Then why are you interested?"

Thys turned around. "Consider what Klein is. What he represents. If nothing else, he's too big."

"How big?"

"We have no idea. That's part of the problem."

"Can't you make a rough estimate?"

"It would be academic. He is undoubtedly using leverage. In fact, *vast* amounts of leverage. The assets that he controls will be many times larger than his capital."

"Doesn't he have to file regulatory returns?"

Thys shook his head. "Atracor Capital isn't registered as an investment advisor in any of the main jurisdictions."

"But that would be illegal."

"It all depends on who his clients are. We have no idea. In fact, we don't even know if he has any clients at all. We presume, given his size, that he must be using other people's money in addition to his own. We presume, given his reputation in the market, that he must have a huge number of clients. But we have no way of knowing for sure."

"Why don't you ask him?"

Thys dusted his lapel, as though he were removing something distasteful. "We've tried to engage Klein in dialogue on many occasions."

"And?"

"What do you think? We've got nowhere."

"Can't you subpoena him?"

"On what grounds? In which jurisdiction? He's not breaking any laws that we know of."

"What do you want me to do?"

"We believe that Atracor Capital is controlled from its offices in St James. I understand that you've had experience in the London markets. We'd like you to go back there, and make enquiries."

"What do you want to know?"

Thys walked up to the desk, tapping the ash from his cigarette into the waste basket. "Let's take a step back for a moment, and consider the big picture. You can see what's happening in the markets, but there's more to it than meets the eye. We're getting some bad signals from the derivatives market in particular. People in the know are worried. Specifically the people in credit default swaps. There are problems with collateral, such that some parts of the market have started to seize up.

But we're not getting a complete picture, and that's the problem. The derivatives market is so massive and so fragmented, that it's impossible to take a view of it in totality. We're just getting scraps here and there, and we're trying to piece them together. But they tell us we should be worried. *Very* worried."

Thys turned back to the window, as though he were surveying what he was describing. "For a long time now, regulators have been finding it nearly impossible to figure out who is behind most derivatives activity. Hedge funds and principal traders are almost all privately held, and operate with minimal supervision. There are now so many places where financial instruments are traded, that nobody has clarity of supply and demand.

It's getting to the point where financial markets are failing in their primary role, which is to provide an accurate and transparent price discovery mechanism." He turned back to me, taking another draw on his cigarette. "In fact, we've already reached the point where there's a complete breakdown in investor trust in the way markets work.

The man in the street has been burned so many times that it's natural for him to take the view that everything is rigged against him. We can't have that. We need to look him in the eye and tell him that the market is fair. Right now, we are not able to do that." Thys paused, watching me as if he was expecting an answer.

"You're holding Klein responsible for the failings of the financial system?"

"I am giving you context. Klein is at the heart of that context."

"What do you want to know, specifically?"

Thys smiled. "Everything. Everything about Klein, and Atracor Capital."

"Can you be a little more exact?"

"We want to know the size of his funds, how much leverage he's using, what his daily turnover is. What instruments he's trading, and where he's doing it." Thys paused, inspecting the tip of the cigarette.

"But to get to the heart of it, you need to get to know Klein. All the information we have on him is out of date. What kind of a man has he become? What is his motivation? What is his ultimate goal? We'd like to know all of that." Thys took another draw on his cigarette and slowly released its smoke into the air between us. "Ideally, we want you to engage him. Maybe you could even bring him in."

"Bring him in?"

"Into dialogue with us, and our members. People like Klein are too important to be on the outside, doing their own thing."

"You want me to knock on Atracor's door and ask to see him?"

Thys shook his head. "We want you to start at a distance. You need to be as discreet as possible. And you would need to start immediately. Time is of the essence." He stubbed out his cigarette in a coffee cup and stood watching me, arms folded. "So? What do you think?"

"It would be tough. The information you're looking for has value, and people aren't just going to volunteer it. The world doesn't work like that."

"There's always plenty of market gossip."

"And that's all it is, gossip. Hearsay which people give away, because it's worthless."

"What would you suggest?"

"I'd start with Atracor's prime broker. They'll have the best view of his trades and his overall exposure."

Thys nodded. "We're on the same page then."

"But they'll never volunteer any information. They won't even speak to me. I'd need nothing less than a subpoena."

Thys smiled, glancing at his colleagues. "A hedge fund like Atracor may be beyond our grasp, but their prime broker is not. Certainly not when it is one of the world's largest investment banks."

"You can compel them to provide the information?"

"We can suggest it."

"I thought you didn't want any mention of the BIS in this."

"That's why you will be doing it. But before we go any further, are you interested in what I am proposing?"

I didn't give it much thought at all. "Yes," I said.

"Very well." Thys slid a dossier across the desk. "Take the day off and have a look at this. Give us a call in the morning if you want to proceed. But before you go, you will need to sign this." He held out a piece of paper.

"What is it?"

"A confidentiality agreement."

One of the men handed me a pen. I signed."

"Hold on," said Jongstra. "By telling us your story, you're breaking the agreement."

Carraway smiled. "Maybe it's not covered by that."

"But if you divulge confidential information, it makes us party to anything that could result-"

"Look around you," said Valassis as he reached for the humidor on the deck locker. "What good is a contract here?"

Jongstra turned to me. "You're a lawyer. What do you think?"

"He has a point. It would be hard to enforce that contract here in Vietnam. In any case, a confidentiality agreement is overridden by matters of public interest." I looked at Carraway. "Is that it? Is your story a matter of public interest?"

He smiled again. "That depends on what public it is."

"It's his problem anyway," said Valassis as he took out a cigar. "Not ours." He bit the end off and lit it, puffing out a clump of smoke in Carraway's direction. "What are you waiting for? Get on with it."

"I signed the agreement. Thys folded it up and put it in his jacket pocket. He was about to leave the office, but then he turned back to me. "Klein may be the smartest man in the business, but he doesn't walk on water. It doesn't matter how clever he is, or how much money he controls. At the end of the day, we have the greatest power and influence."

Thys left the office, his two colleagues following behind.

I picked up the dossier and took an elevator to the ground floor, walking out into that cold February morning. You would think the BIS's headquarters would be discreetly tucked away somewhere, but they're housed in an office tower in front of Basel's main railway station. The city's trams pull up right alongside. It's a very convenient place if you're arriving by public transport, but the world's central bankers never arrive by public transport.

From my office I could see the Rhine, cutting Basel in two. I could see France on the west bank and Germany on the east bank, but you'd never know as there's nothing to demarcate the border. Nothing to say that two separate countries are just a couple of kilometres away. Just like you'd never know that quiet town of Basel lies at the heart of so much."

4

"I hadn't been back to London for a couple of years. Everything was old and familiar, yet at the same time it felt like I'd been left behind.
On the face of it, London was booming. I stayed in a brand new hotel which had preserved the façade of the Victorian boarding house that had been demolished to make way for it. The scale of the rooms was more American than European, but somehow the architect had managed to line them up with the windows of those little box rooms they had replaced.

My meeting wasn't in the traditional financial district, the City of London. Since the late eighties, the big banks have been migrating to Canary Wharf with its huge office towers and lower rents. In order to compete, the City dropped most planning requirements so that it could put up glass towers of its own along its quaint medieval lanes.

I looked out from my taxi at a skyline bristling with construction cranes. My father used to say that cranes are a perfect barometer. The more there are, the more likely you're at the peak of a boom and therefore closer to recession.

I arrived late, not realising how bad the traffic would be. I was shown to a meeting room on the fourteenth floor of a building that had no thirteenth. Although they don't like to admit it, bankers are a superstitious lot.

Even though I was late, they made me wait quite some time. It was mid afternoon, but the February sun was low in the sky, shining straight into the room.

I went to the window and looked out. The only river traffic passing Canary Wharf these days are tourist boats heading to Greenwich and garbage scows heading to Essex. You can still see the old docks, which handled the incredible share of world trade on which London's wealth was built. That's long gone, but it has been replaced by an even more valuable share of global financial flows.

I watched the Thames sparkling below me, a ribbon threaded through the city like an adornment. At high tide you could be mistaken for thinking that you're looking at the start of a great river, but it's just the end of an estuary. When the tide is out the Thames is more mud-bank than river, complete with shopping trolleys and traffic cones poking out of the muck. The water is usually a greyish brown, but that afternoon it shone, courtesy of the low winter sun. Like tarnished silver given a hasty shine."

"Remind me," said Jongstra. "Who were you seeing?"

"Atracor's Prime Broker." Carraway looked around at us. "Does everyone here know what that is?"

Nobody replied.

"Fund managers generally use a stockbroker, an external administrator and a custodian. Hedge funds typically use prime brokers, which provide most of those services bundled together, including stock lending and credit. It follows that they have the best insight into what their hedge fund clients are doing." Carraway paused, looking at Valassis. "Do you mind if I have another beer?"

"Take whatever's in the bucket. When it's gone, it's gone."

Carraway reached for a beer from the ice bucket and cracked its tab. "After I'd waited for almost half an hour, a man walked in wearing a buttoned-up suit. We shook hands and I gave him my card. He was shorter than me, and motioned for me to sit down.

He picked up a bottle of water from a drinks trolley next to the door. "What's this about?" he said, unscrewing the cap and drinking from the bottle.

"I presume my email was fairly self-explanatory. I'd like to discuss one of your clients."

"And who would that be?" he said, even though I had stated it in my email.

"Atracor Capital."

He frowned, walking up to the table. "What exactly is the nature of your enquiry?"

"We're looking for background. Anything you can tell us, that would help-"

"*We*?" he said, examining my card in his hand.

"The BIS. The Financial Stability Board in particular, which is a new secretariat-"

"And you?"

"I work for them."

He looked at me for a few moments, slowly rubbing my card between his thumb and forefinger. I had no title. That clearly bothered him. "What exactly is it that you do there?"

"Special projects, like this."

"And what is the nature of this 'special project'?"

"We want to be as discreet about it as possible, but basically we're trying to understand more about current activity in the derivatives markets. We're specifically interested in the big hedge funds. Given Atracor's scale and importance, it's obvious that we would start with them."

He gave a half smile, taking another swig of water. "And you came to me."

I nodded. "As their prime broker."

"Who is interested in keeping his clients. So give me one good reason why I would want to piss off Atracor Capital by talking to the likes of you."

"We have influence."

His eyes narrowed. "And what is that supposed to mean?"

"Our members are your regulators."

"What exactly are you getting at? We're within the law. You want to investigate us? Get a warrant."

"This isn't an investigation. We just want some background on Atracor, and we think that you can help."

"Have you people never heard of client confidentiality? Do you really think I'm going to spill the beans about my clients to every Tom, Dick and Harry?"

"We are not every Tom, Dick and Harry."

"So what are you then? What is it that you people actually do in Zurich?"

"We're in Basel. Our chief concern is the stability of the market."

He frowned, looking down at me. The table between us reflected the sunlight into our faces. "What exactly is there to be concerned about?"

"It's obvious."

"*Really?*" He smiled. "Explain it to me."

"There are some serious dislocations in the markets. Almost everywhere you look, volatility levels are through the roof."

"And what's wrong with that?"

"It's in everyone's interests to have stable markets."

He smiled again, shaking his head. "That proves you people in Basel know next to nothing."

I was about to speak, but he put up his hand, cutting me short. "Volatility is the lifeblood of this business. It is a pulse. It's evidence that the markets are alive and kicking. All you regulators want to do is sit on them, squashing the life out of them." He finished the water and tossed the bottle into a waste bin. He had my card in the same hand, so I presume that went in too.

"If your bosses in Basel want to find out what's causing this volatility, the answer is we all are. This is what it's about. It's called capitalism, and it works. You wouldn't have a salary if it wasn't for us. Be thankful for that, and leave us to get on with the real work." He glanced at his watch. "I have a meeting."

He walked out the room, leaving the door open behind him."

Carraway stopped as the yacht swayed, bumping against the fenders on the quay. The tide was starting to lift the hull from the mud bank. The river seemed even busier in the late afternoon, matched by the stream of tuk-tuks and scooters that buzzed along the quay.

The deck was several feet below the level of the quayside, reducing our view of the passing traffic to a mass of wheels and legs criss-crossing each other beneath the boat's awning.

Most of the street hawkers had given up on us long ago, but two young women remained. They squatted on the edge of the quay, watching us underneath the awning. Their baskets rested on the concrete, but they kept the bamboo poles across their shoulders as if they needed to jump up and offer us their wares at a moment's notice.

It looked uncomfortable sitting for so long in that position, but at least the shade from our awning was coming their way as the sun slipped lower.

Carraway asked if I would shift along the bench, so he could get out of the sun. As I moved, the women stood up expectantly, but I was careful not to make eye contact and they settled back down again. Carraway reached for his beer and took a sip before continuing.

"I left their office, walking out into the shadow of the building. It was mid afternoon on a beautiful sunny day, but it was bitterly cold and there was hardly anyone about. I called the office from my mobile, telling Thys what had happened. He didn't sound surprised, telling me to call back in the morning.

I had to return to Canary Wharf that evening, as I'd arranged to meet an old friend for a drink. I knew Glenn from my London days, largely because we'd both ended up in investment banks by accident. Back then he was an academic at heart, recently graduated with a Masters in molecular biology. Now he was trading derivatives, and doing very well out of it.

There are supposed to be so-called 'Chinese walls' within investment banks, to avoid the inherent conflict of interest between brokers acting on behalf of their clients, and proprietary traders who trade the market for the bank's own account. Everyone knows those Chinese walls are bogus, with information on client order flows regularly finding its way to the traders, for the bank's benefit. As such, Glenn was in a position to see a lot of what the big hedge funds were doing in the derivatives market.

He was late, as always. I should have remembered that. I ended up waiting for almost an hour. The bar was packed with after-work drinkers. Everyone in that bar wore a suit and they were all young and attractive, especially after a few drinks. In spite of the jitters in the markets, money was flowing freely around me.

After a couple of beers I felt a buzz I hadn't encountered in a long time. I was surprised at the wave of nostalgia flowing through me. I looked around, wondering if I knew anyone there. I started talking with a group of women who were out celebrating. It was either a promotion, or someone was leaving. I can't remember which.

When Glenn finally arrived, I didn't recognise him. He had put on weight and lost most of his hair. He didn't look good at all, and he was only thirty-four. But he was doing well, really well, just like all those people in that bar. The stress of the job had clearly taken a higher toll on him than anyone else there, and maybe that's why he seemed to hold them all in quiet contempt.

He glanced around the bar as if it was all beneath him. "Why did you choose this place?"

"It's the only one I could remember."

"It's full of secretaries."

"That was never a problem for you."

"Times change." He flashed his wedding ring. "What are you in town for? An audit?"

I shook my head. "We don't do audits."

"Who do you work for again?"

"The BIS."

"I read something about them, the other day. Can't remember what it was."

"Couldn't have been too interesting then."

He smiled. "Remind me why you signed up with them."

"I wanted to try something different."

Glenn shook his head. "Backpacking around the world is different. If you want to find yourself, go to Asia. Don't go to Basel." He eyed the group of secretaries for a few moments, and then turned back to me. "'B' people work for regulators. 'A' people stay here, in the real world." He glanced across the bar, clicking his fingers.

"How are things?" I asked.

"*Things?*"

"How's business?"

"Could be better. Choppy waters, very choppy. But we're fine. Compared to some of the others. They're being carried out."

"Carried out?"

"Finished, dead. Game over."

"Is it serious?"

Glenn shrugged. "In a way it's a good thing. We need markets like these to separate the men from the boys. The past few years, everyone's had it easy. Complete idiots have been making far too much money." He turned to the bar. "Hey! How about some service here?"

A bartender looked up from the cocktail he was preparing, giving a nod of acknowledgement. Glenn turned back to me. "So what exactly are you doing here?"

"It's confidential."

His face tightened with interest. "What do you mean?"

"Just a survey," I said, realising my mistake.

"Of what?"

"Hedge funds."

He smiled. "What is it with you people? You're terrified of hedge funds."

"What do you mean, 'you people'?"

"Regulators. That's you. That's what you do now, right?"

"We're not a regulator. We just want to ensure that the system runs smoothly."

He laughed. "What 'system' are you talking about? Have you forgotten everything? There's no such thing as a system. It's a jungle. It works so well *because* it's a jungle. Forget systems, if you want to create even a fraction of the wealth you see around you. You want it to run smoothly? It runs like a fucking dream if you leave it alone." He paused for a moment, watching the secretaries out of the corner of his eye. "Don't you see? You're fighting a losing battle."

"What do you mean?"

"I can trade anywhere I like. In the US alone there are nine exchanges and plenty of other places, including networks run by brokers and banks. Hell, most of the liquidity these days doesn't go though exchanges at all. Dark Pools are popping up all over the place. No one can keep a handle on it. Give up, you're wasting your time."

"Can you back up for a moment?" said Jongstra.

Carraway turned to him. "What is it?"

"Some of those terms you're using. What do you mean by 'liquidity' and 'pools'?"

"Trading terms," said Valassis.

"That's right," nodded Carraway. "Liquidity is the rate at which transactions occur in a particular market. If it's liquid then it's functioning well, with a healthy transaction flow. Liquidity is vital for any market. Without it, everything seizes up; there's no accurate price for anything. A market economy can't function.

And then you get 'dark pools'. For some time now, liquidity has been sucked away from regulated banks and exchanges. Transactions are being executed in places called dark pools where they can't be seen or measured by outsiders. You could say they're like black holes, in that they're only measurable by their impact on everything else." Carraway took a sip of beer, glancing at Valassis. "But before our host reminds me that I'm digressing, let me get back to the story."

"I let Glenn spout on for a bit, stroking his ego, wondering why we were ever friends. Finally the bartender came over and I ordered a couple of beers.

"Make it proper drink," said Glenn.

"How about a Martini?"

He laughed. "Jesus, where've you been all this time?"

I ignored him, ordering two vodka Martinis from the bartender.

"Make sure it's Chopin," said Glenn.

The bartender replied that they didn't stock Chopin vodka.

"What did I tell you about this place?" Glenn tossed a black Amex card on the counter. "Make it Grey Goose. And open a tab."

"The vodka makes no difference," I said. "You're drinking it with a mixer."

"It'll make a difference to your hangover."

"It's just snob appeal."

Glenn laughed. "You want to talk snob appeal? Have you heard of the ten thousand dollar Martini?"

I shook my head.

"They sell it at the Algonquin Hotel in New York. It's called the 'Martini on the Rock'. In this case, the rock is not an ice-cube. It's a diamond at the bottom of the glass."

"That's ridiculous."

He smiled, shaking his head. It was clear to him that I was completely out of touch. "One of our client dinners can easily cost twice that amount. At the end of the day, it's all about marketing. Like the two hundred dollar hamburger on Wall Street. It has gold dusting on the bun."

"Are you serious?"

He nodded. "As long as someone will pay for it, give it to them." His Blackberry pinged in his pocket and he took it out, scrolling through the messages. "Which hedge funds are you investigating?" he said, without looking up.

"It's not an investigation."

"Okay. Which funds are you *interested* in?"

"Just the big ones."

"Like who?"

"Atracor Capital." I couldn't resist.

He frowned, returning the Blackberry to his pocket. "They've agreed to see you?"

"Not yet."

"You won't get anything on them. You realise that, right?"

"We'll see. I've only just started."

He shook his head. "You're not listening to me. You'll get nothing from Atracor. *Nothing*. Got it?"

I shrugged. "Do you know anything about them?"

He laughed, but I could see he was flattered. "*I'm* your source?"

"Right now, anything you know would be helpful."

"Information like that has value. Nobody's going to give it away for free."

"But we're friends, right?"

He gave me a half-smile. "We were. Then you went off to Switzerland to work for a bunch of bureaucrats. Tell me, what do you believe in these days?"

"What do you mean?"

"We used to be on the same page. Now I'm not so sure."

"Like I said, I'm trying something different."

He shook his head. "You regulators are out to get as much control as you can. You're obsessed with it. Look around, look how well the City's doing. Why? One simple answer. Light regulation. Let people get on with it, don't choke everything with red tape."

He paused, reaching for a Martini as the bartender set them down on the counter. "Can't you see what's going on? Those bureaucrats you work for are green with envy because we're making money hand over fist. So what if the rich get richer? It's not a zero sum game. These aren't the days of Robin Hood. If you want to get rich, you don't have to steal from anyone.

As long as everyone's making money, who cares? So what if the guys at the top are pulling down stratospheric amounts? It's just envy, nothing more. I have the freedom to earn as much money as I want, and no one is going to take that away from me." He winced as he took a sip from the glass. "That is not Grey Goose."

I shrugged.

"Taste it. You'll see."

"I wouldn't know the difference."

He shook his head, clicking his fingers. When the bartender responded, he made him replace both drinks.

"Why are we having Martinis anyway?" he said as the bartender took them away.

"You didn't want beer."

"That doesn't mean I want a fucking Martini. These days I'm on Champagne."

"Champagne?"

He nodded. "Krug. But they won't have it here."

"How do you know?"

"It's fucking obvious." He watched the bartender pouring our drinks down the sink. "I was in Saint Moritz a week ago, and some Russian oligarchs were shaking bottles of vintage Krug and spraying the crowd. Then a bunch of Americans did it with Laurent-Perrier, and they were booed."

I let the conversation drift after that. We had a good few Martinis, which Glenn didn't complain about again. Finally, I brought him back to the subject of Atracor. This time he was much more ready to talk.

"They're based in St James, but Klein is never seen coming or going. In fact, he's never seen in public."

"Why?" I asked.

"Klein's obsessed with secrecy. In any case, he doesn't have to come into the office at all. He can do everything remotely. I wouldn't be in London in February if I could avoid it. I'd find a nice beach in the Caribbean."

"How do you think he's generating his returns?"

"He's using every trick in the book. He's doing anything he likes, because he can."

"Like what?"

"No doubt you've heard of his fabled algorithms, right?"

I nodded.

"As I was just saying, there are lots of different trading platforms. He's using his algorithms to trade between them, arbitraging the price differentials. And when you're someone of Klein's scale, you can do even more. You can make everything come your way."

"How so?"

"It's called 'quote stuffing'. You pump a shit-load of orders through an exchange, which you almost immediately cancel. As a result, that exchange will run fractionally slower than the rest of the market, leaving you to cherry-pick delayed quotes and play them off against quotes on other platforms that haven't been delayed." He finished his Martini and put the glass down on the bar. "And Klein's in cahoots with plenty of market-makers. They let him see the order flow coming through from the market, and he gives them a piece of the action. It's a win-win situation."

"For them, not the market."

Glenn laughed. "What is the market?"

"What do you mean?"

"Can I be any clearer? *We* are the fucking market. Everyone's doing it."

"But if everyone does it, why is he so far ahead?"

"As I said, he doesn't have to answer to anyone. None of you fucking regulators. And the guy is using scale, okay? Fucking massive scale. We couldn't do that. The prop trading desks at any bank have strict risk limits, but hedge funds like Atracor don't have to give a shit about that. He's so fucking big, he can throw as much as he likes at the markets. They go whichever way he wants them to."

"You're pretty sure Klein's doing that? Quote stuffing?"

Glenn nodded.

"How do you know? How do you know for certain that's what he does?"

"Everyone knows. *Everyone*."

I didn't get much else from him that night. It was comforting, in a way. I'd left the City a few years previously and Glenn had stayed on, busting a gut for his career and doing really well out of it. Yet he couldn't tell me much more than I already knew."

"Or wouldn't," said Jongstra.

"Yes, indeed." Carraway took a sip of beer, swilling it around in his mouth. "I sucked up his arrogance and his vanity, figuring that I might need him. I let him pay for the drinks, and said it would be good to see him again."

Carraway watched the two street hawkers on the quayside for a few moments. Until then, had any of us made eye contact they would have raised their baskets, calling out to us. But now they just stared at him. They knew they weren't going to make a sale, but at the same time were reluctant to leave these four white men on whom they had pinned their hopes all afternoon. The fruit in their baskets had been sitting in the sun all day.

Carraway turned back to us. "I had a hangover the next morning. Maybe Glenn had been right about the vodka. I woke to find a message on my phone. Thys wanted me to go back to the prime broker. He would be more cooperative this time.

A meeting had been arranged that evening. People work long hours in investment banks, but eight o'clock was a strange time for it.

The traffic had eased up a lot after seven, but something in me made me want to arrive late. I walked around Canary Wharf for twenty minutes, looking into the crowded restaurants and bars. I went past the bar I had been in the night before. Everyone in there looked the same.

I walked across to the bank's offices. Most of the people had gone home, but all the lights were on. The steel and glass tower was a goldfish bowl in the night sky, with all its floors on display.

The receptionists were off duty, but a security guard directed me to a meeting room on the fourteenth floor. I hadn't expected to be back there so soon. I guess the BIS does have some influence after all.

I was only there a couple of minutes when the same man who met me the day before appeared. He wasn't wearing a suit jacket, and his shirtsleeves were rolled up.

"Just what is it that you people want?" he said, closing the door behind him.

"I told you yesterday."

"Run it by me again."

"We want to find out more about Atracor Capital. In particular, Klein. You don't have to divulge anything behind his back. Ideally, if you could get me a meeting with him-"

"And what makes you think I have any influence at all with Klein?"

"You're his prime broker."

The man turned to the window. It reflected the light of the room, a black mirror that captured the dark image of him standing there. "Did it ever occur to you people that your information is old?"

I looked at him. "What do you mean?"

He continued watching the window. "I don't want this getting out into the market."

"There's no reason why it should."

He turned around, looking at me for a few moments. "We haven't seen a penny of business from Klein for years."

"But you're his prime broker."

He shook his head. "Not anymore."

"He pulled the business?"

"That's pretty fucking obvious, wouldn't you say?"

"Do you know who he went to?"

"Do you know anything about this business? Hedge funds like Atracor don't use just one prime broker, they use several. They spread it around."

"But you're one of the largest brokers in the industry."

"*The* largest. But we're not even one of several, as far as Klein is concerned."

"Why did he take the business away?"

"How should I know? Do you really think he would tell us?" The man stood watching me. "Happy now?"

Before I could reply, he turned and walked away. "This better not get out into the market," he said, opening the door.

As he walked out of the room, he looked back. "You won't get to see Klein. Nobody gets to see Klein. I never did, and Atracor was my account. Nobody sees Klein, unless he wants to see them."

5

"So you had a problem," I said.

Carraway nodded. "I had a problem."

The boat juddered as it came down on its keel, lifted by a swell in the river. The air was absolutely still, filled with the buzz of passing boats and the rattle of scooters and tuk-tuks on the quayside.

"What did you do?" asked Jongstra.

"Basel arranged a meeting for me with the UK regulator, the Financial Services Authority. They were polite, but not much help. Regulators are by their nature territorial, and don't exactly welcome interlopers on their patch. They didn't like that my purpose for being there was cloudy at best. After all, they're supposed to have suspicious minds. I left with nothing other than vague promises of assistance, the kind you get from people who want to get rid of you as quickly as possible.

But I walked out of there relieved that I wasn't going to be wasting any more time with them. They clearly didn't have a clue what was going on.

All the European markets had big falls that week. With just a few trading days left, February was going to be another down month. People were especially rattled by that."

"Why?" I asked.

"It's called the 'January effect.' Stockmarkets almost always start the year in positive territory. If you look at the historical data, in the very few years where that isn't the case, markets end up very badly."

"Are stockmarkets really that simplistic?"

Carraway shrugged. "Stockmarkets are nothing more than mass psychology. And humans are, at the end of the day, simplistic beings. January is the beginning of a new year. New resolutions, expectations of a clean start and all that stuff. It's like gym attendance, always higher in January than in subsequent months.

Anyway, when I was leaving the FSA I got a call from Basel. This time it wasn't Thys, it was someone else calling on his behalf. He had a proposition for me. He was very careful in the way he phrased it, suggesting that I could pose as a prospective investor."

"Is that allowed?" asked Jongstra.

Carraway took a sip of beer before answering. "Put it this way. When it comes to a hedge fund like Atracor, pretty much anything is allowed."

"I don't buy that argument. If you're setting the rules, you've got to stick within them."

Carraway shook his head. "Atracor was beyond everything. There were no rules, period."

"Hey!" shouted Valassis. Something had caught his eye and he stood up, leaning over the gunwale. "Get out of here!"

A barge that was attempting to come alongside the quay had swung in too close to the yacht and was about to collide. We all stood up.

Three crew members ran to the side of the barge, slapping their hands against the yacht's hull. They pushed hard, heads down and muscles taut across their bare shoulders, with Valassis screaming down at them.

The barge had come to a virtual standstill, but as they pushed it slowly began to swing away, its bow turning out into the river. The crew looked up at us, breathing heavily with their arms at their sides, while we held our beers and Valassis continued to berate them.

Finally he turned around and we sat back down.

"And?" I asked. "You agreed to do it?"

Carraway nodded. "By the following week, I had a serviced office in London and a set of business cards that said very little. I was representing a Family Office, the most secretive of wealth managers. Family Offices are set up to manage the finances of extremely well-off families, maintaining a veil to keep them hidden from the outside world.

My first stop was Geneva. I'd arranged a meeting with a private bank who were known to operate one of the biggest feeder funds to Atracor Capital. I won't use their real name, so let's just call them Banque Privé.

Like Basel, Geneva is a protestant city and everything appears subdued and austere. But a huge amount of wealth is concentrated there, in the hands of Geneva's private banks. It spills out into the city's fashionable restaurants and bars, which are packed with an international glitterati who have followed their money and are only too happy to flaunt it.

I arrived in early March, but it felt like spring was well underway. Geneva has a great location at the head of Lac Leman, where the Rhone flows into France. The private banks are all clustered along its south bank, each with a blank facade. Banque Privé's headquarters has no polished brass plaques, nothing to say what lies within.

Once you are inside, the receptionist doesn't ask your name, and certainly won't ask for a business card. I had a meeting with a Swiss-Italian, a man called Domenico. All I had to do was mention his name, and I was escorted to a meeting room on the first floor.

I was left in an impeccably decorated chamber, bouncing on my heels on the thickly piled carpet while I inspected the art on the walls. I'd never heard of any of the artists, but their paintings looked reliably expensive.

Domenico appeared soundlessly through a side door. He was immaculately groomed, and very well tanned for the end of winter. Everything about him spoke of years of client service at a private bank.

He shook my hand, thanking me for coming. Geneva is the home of the world's finest watchmakers, and yet there was a Swatch on his wrist. As a local, I guess he knew that Swatch makes the movements for most Swiss watches, so if you buy an Omega or a Breguet or a Longines, underneath it all you're actually buying a Swatch.

I didn't offer any explanation of who I was. If anything, it was helpful that this private banker had never heard of me or the office that I represented. In the private banking world, where the greatest wealth is the quietest, anonymity is not a weakness but a strength. I made allusions that my client was Middle Eastern. With the price of oil over one hundred dollars a barrel, what more needed to be said?

I went on to explain that my office was dissatisfied with the performance of its existing funds, and that I was scouting for new managers. Domenico remained almost inscrutable, but I could tell he was pleased to hear that. What's sweeter than the prospect of taking business from a rival?

We talked a bit about the funds on offer at Banque Privé. Atracor Capital was not mentioned. I sat through Domenico's spiel on their 'recommended' managers before finally broaching the subject.

Domenico paused and gave a very slight smile, as though I needed humouring. "Atracor Capital has been closed to new clients for some years now. Even existing clients have to join the queue if they want to make additional contributions."

"But you operate one of their largest feeder funds. Surely you must have some influence with Klein?"

Domenico coughed politely. "We would prefer to talk about Atracor Capital."

"I thought we were."

Domenico shook his head. "Dr Klein doesn't like anyone using his name."

"I understand. But don't you have some influence with them?"

He nodded. "On behalf of our clients, of course."

The emphasis was on clients, which obviously I was not. Not yet. The line had been cast.

I readily took the bait. "That's good to hear. My office is prepared to invest a significant amount of capital. The family is a long-term investor who would remain committed-"

Domenico gave me a patient smile. "The Atracor fund is closed. It has reached its optimal size. If it grew any further, it could negatively impact returns to existing clients." He reopened the brochure he had put in front of me. "As I was explaining, we have many excellent hedge funds, several of them exclusive to ourselves. The fact that we are the most significant Atracor client reflects just how effective we are at selecting star managers. We have been with Atracor right from the start." He offered me his broadest smile as he pushed the brochure closer. "No doubt the next Atracor will be among those funds that we currently offer."

I let him run through the rest of his sales pitch. Some of the funds he was peddling had returns similar to Atracor, but none had been going for as long. As I reminded Domenico, a month is a long time in the hedge fund world and longevity has a premium.

"Which is why Atracor is so popular," he replied.

I closed the brochure and sat back in my chair. "My client is particularly set on Atracor Capital, and nothing will dissuade him. He is prepared to pay double your usual commission to get in."

Domenico shook his head. "It is not up to us. It is for Atracor to decide."

"But you've just admitted that you have influence. As their largest client-"

Domenico frowned, as though I was putting him in a difficult position. He looked down, brushing invisible dust from the table. "What kind of commitment would your client be interested in making?"

"In the range of three hundred million," I said, plucking a figure out of the air.

Domenico looked up, retaining his air of inscrutability. It was impossible to say whether he was impressed at all. "Swiss Francs?" he said.

I nodded. He was after all taking business from a rival.

He sat looking at me for a few moments, tapping his finger on the brochure I had rejected. For a moment I thought he had seen right though me, but then he sat forward, clasping his hands together. "If Atracor does open to new investors, we can do our utmost to ensure that you are in the queue. But you must understand that many of our long-standing clients have been waiting years for access."

"As I said, my client is prepared to double your upfront commission."

Domenico smiled again. "We do not charge upfront commissions." He pushed the brochure towards me once more. "When you have time, take a look at our fee schedule. It's all in there."

We left it at that, both with baited hooks. He with the understanding that I would consider their wider offering, me with the understanding that maybe someday I could get access to Atracor."

"Can I stop you for a moment?" said Jongstra.

"Of course," said Carraway, taking advantage of the interruption to have a sip of beer.

"Why would anyone close a fund?"

"Two reasons. The first is that the larger a fund becomes, the harder it is to outperform the market. It's that issue of liquidity we were talking about earlier. The bigger you are, the less flexibility you have. Like a supertanker trying to manoeuvre in a narrow channel. The smaller boats can whiz around you." He finished his beer and put the can down. "And then there's the second reason, which of course no one would ever admit to. The idea of the 'velvet rope'."

"Which is?"

"Just like a rope across the entrance to a night club. Nothing does more for a fund's marketing than to announce that you're closed to new business. The illusion of exclusivity, of scarce supply, of getting into a club that no one else can get into. It's irresistible to new investors."

"Even professionals?" I asked.

Carraway nodded. "Even professionals. In fact, especially professionals. The industry is all about perception. Scratch beneath the surface, and you might be shocked at what you find."

"You're right about that," said Jongstra. "My broker's lost me a ton of money. He saw none of this coming."

Carraway shook his head. "That's not his job. His job is to sell you stuff."

"He's still got to do right by his clients. He can't just load them up with crap. That's unethical, if not downright illegal."

"Not necessarily. Your broker is out to make money, just like you are, and he makes money by selling you stuff. He doesn't make money by telling you to hold off and wait. And because stock markets generally go up over time, he can say in good faith that it'll all work out at the end of the day."

Jongstra shook his head. "I'm in a business where if we don't perform, we're finished. No one would ever hire us again. You can't tell me that these guys-"

"You hired him, didn't you?" said Carraway.

"Yes, I did," said Jongstra.

"And even after he burned you, he's still in business?"

"I believe he is."

Carraway smiled. "Enough said. That's the finance world for you. Quite unlike anything else. Tell me, what exactly did your broker do that he shouldn't have?"

"He sold me stocks that crashed."

"If he could work out in advance which way the market was about to go, he'd be doing it for himself. Not for you. The reason why he's selling you stuff is because he *can't* work it out for himself."

"The answer is simple," said Valassis. He hadn't spoken for some time, and we all looked at him.

"Get a good broker. Mine is excellent. He's proved his worth many times over."

"Care to recommend him?" I said.

Valassis took a draw on his cigar, letting the smoke slip up into the still air. "As Carraway said, if you already know the best, why tell anyone?" He glanced at his watch and turned back to Carraway. "So you knocked on a few doors and got nowhere. Unless you want your story to go nowhere, I suggest you speed it up."

"After Banque Privé I had a meeting with a rival bank in Geneva, who were also known to run an Atracor feeder fund. We knew they had a suffered a lot of withdrawals in the German and Italian tax amnesties, so they would presumably be receptive to the prospect of a big new client.

But the response I got from them was more or less the same. These guys were clearly more eager than Banque Privé and were keen to help, but they admitted that they couldn't do anything on that front. Atracor was quite simply closed to new business.

So I went back to London empty-handed. I spent the rest of that week going to see some of the big fund-of-funds in the city. These outfits gather money specifically for investment in hedge funds. They claim to use their expertise to sift through all the thousands of funds, many of them very opaque with virtually no public information, selecting the best in which to invest their clients' money. For that they layer on a similar fee to what the hedge funds themselves charge.

But the funds that were able to say anything about Atracor all said the same thing. It was off the radar.

By the end of the week, I had nothing to show for my efforts. Basel were increasingly impatient. Stockmarkets had continued to slide, and it was the banks and insurance companies that were taking the biggest hits. A falling stock price isn't great for any company, but for a bank it's especially bad. It can very easily become fatal.

"How so?" I asked.

"As I said before, the finance industry is all about perception. Banks stand in the middle of a chain of borrowing and lending in which everyone assumes that everyone else is good for the money. A sinking stock price alerts clients and counterparties to the possibility that maybe someone knows something about this bank which they don't. Maybe there's a break in the chain. That can make them pull their exposure, which then leads to a domino effect, creating a run on the bank.

One bank in particular was being singled out. Schwartz Greenberg wasn't a tier one investment bank, but was nevertheless still a major player. They were into mortgage-backed securities in a big way, and it was rumoured that a lot of that business had gone bad. Hedge funds were having a field day, knowing that they couldn't lose. The more they hammered the stock price, the weaker it became, and with that the more likely the bank was to collapse.

Like predators picking off the weak from the rest of the herd, they were hammering Schwartz Greenberg's stock lower and lower. There were rumours that Atracor in particular was targeting the bank. In the dossier that Thys had given me there was an interview with Klein from some fifteen years ago, where he showed contempt for the banks, and a particular enmity for Schwartz Greenberg.

Schwartz had asserted many times that everything was fine, but hadn't done anything to prove it. To be fair, they couldn't. If they had been able to say 'We have these three bond issues and they're all okay', they would have been fine. But they had thousands of bond issues, backed by millions of mortgages that had been originated by someone else and pooled together by someone else. Some of it was insured, but it wasn't clear who the underwriters were, and whether they were still good for it.

And that was just one of Schwartz's many lines of business. Out of that thicket, how can you possibly stand up in front of the world and say 'everything's okay'? Why would anyone believe you?

To make matters worse, banks like Schwartz had been loading up on debt, just like your average man in the street. In financial-speak, it's called 'leverage'. Schwartz were leveraged around thirty times, do you know what that means?" Carraway looked around at us.

Without waiting for a reply, he continued. "If you take out a typical mortgage and put down a thirty percent deposit, then your leverage is just over two times. It's considered especially risky if you put down a ten percent deposit, in which case your leverage is nine times. Schwartz were *thirty* times leveraged. That meant the slightest loss on that haystack of assets on their balance sheet could easily wipe out their capital.

To know with any degree of comfort that their capital was not worthless required a very high degree of precision. But in an environment of such high volatility, that precision simply wasn't there. You just didn't know. So Schwartz very quickly entered a death spiral.

A bank with over sixty billion dollars in capital and tens of thousands of employees unravelled over just a few days. On Wednesday they said everything was fine. But that had ceased to work long ago, because everyone knew they weren't fine. On Thursday they said nothing, as if nothing more needed to be said. That didn't help either. They appeared cavalier. On Friday they said they were fine, and gave even more information to the market. But it could never be enough to restore confidence, and it made them look desperate. Withdrawals started to haemorrhage to such an extent that the Fed stepped in over the weekend.

On Monday it emerged that a larger rival had been 'persuaded' to buy Schwartz Greenberg for less than a dollar a share. They had been trading over one hundred and fifty dollars a year previously.

And it was on that Monday, when I was reading about it in the Financial Times, when I got a call from Domenico. Having learnt something of the game, I pretended not to remember him. It worked like a dream.

He reminded me of my interest in Atracor. He explained that they might have a once-in-a-lifetime opening, but it was confidential. I was to tell no one.

He said he could come and see me in London. He could be there within a few days, if that was convenient. Amazing how things had changed in just a week. The shoe was on the other foot.

I couldn't have him come to see me, so I suggested meeting again in Geneva. When? Maybe a week's time, I said as casually as possible.

It was just as well that I played it cool. A couple of days later I got a call from the other bank that I'd visited, saying that they may have an opening for me. It was very exclusive of course, and they asked that I keep it to myself. In a matter of days, I had gone from nothing to having two very prestigious banks offering me an entry into Atracor."

"Why the U-turn?" asked Jongstra.

"A good question," said Carraway. "If Atracor had been shorting Schwartz as everyone assumed, they should have made a ton of money from its collapse. But a funny thing was happening. A lot of the best fund managers were suffering withdrawals, because people were trying to take profits where they could, to shore up losses elsewhere." Carraway turned to look as the yacht swung to the side, tugging on its bowline. The river had reversed direction and was starting to flow backwards as the incoming tide gathered momentum.

"Lan!" called out Valassis.

We sat in silence, watched by the two street hawkers while scooters and bicycles criss-crossed the quayside behind them.

The woman appeared in the doorway, remaining in the shade while she dried her hands on a cloth.

"Why aren't the crew back yet?"

"She shrugged, saying something unintelligible.

"Go find them. I want them back on the boat, and ready to go in half an hour."

Without replying, she left the cabin and stepped into the sunlight. We watched as she put a foot on the gunwale and then leapt gracefully onto the quayside. The boat was rising with the tide and the gap was smaller than it had been before, but even so, I don't think any of us would have made it without an undignified scramble.

"Do you have to be somewhere?" I asked.

Valassis turned to look at me, as if surprised that I had spoken. "What was that?"

"You seem to be in a rush to get somewhere."

"I want to be out of the Delta by nightfall. There are no channel markers, no lights, no buoys. The sandbars are constantly changing."

"I guess our host has a good reason for leaving," I said, turning back to Carraway. "You'd better get on with your story."

"I went back to Geneva, but this time I didn't want to meet the banks on their turf. I booked into the Hotel Des Bergues, which is an appropriately magnificent place on the lakeshore. I said I would meet them in the foyer. I wanted to appear casual, even off-handish. It mattered so little to me, that I was prepared to discuss a transaction worth hundreds of millions of dollars in a hotel lobby.

I arrived the night before and made full use of the place. It's the best hotel in Geneva, which was helpful for my cover, but in truth the main reason I'd chosen it was because I'd always wanted to stay there. And I had a feeling that I may never have the chance again.

I took breakfast on the patio, overlooking the Jet d'eau out on the lake. It's Geneva's single biggest landmark, a giant fountain that shoots water over a hundred metres high. An incongruous piece of exuberance in Calvin's home town.

I had coffee in the lobby while I waited for Domenico to appear. Geneva is possibly the most international city in the world, and yet I didn't overhear any language other than English that morning.

Domenico arrived bang on time. He had lost some of his inscrutability, as if it had sheared off as he came through the revolving doors. His disposition was a few degrees warmer than before, but he was clearly uncomfortable about my choice of venue. He tactfully suggested a private room. I very casually turned him down.

I strung things out far longer than was necessary, enjoying my chance to dangle bait in the water. He leaned forward in his chair, speaking softly, and I relished his discomfort as I made him repeat himself. I can't hear you, Domenico. Louder. Louder.

He explained that Atracor may have an opening, exclusive to me, in which case it was imperative that I keep it quiet. He advised that I should stand by, with the funds to hand, because we would have to move quickly if the opportunity did in fact arise. Why was never made clear. I should just be grateful that they valued me so much as a prospective client.

Having heard his spiel, I laid out my condition. I wanted to see Klein before I would invest. It's a perfectly acceptable request. A large client will almost always want to see the manager first.

But he refused. "Mr Carraway, as you will no doubt appreciate, our job is much more than simply providing access to a clutch of hedge funds. You came to us because we provide the best managers. All are carefully screened and selected. We undertake all the necessary due diligence and monitoring on your behalf."

"I appreciate that, but I'd still like to see someone from Atracor."

Domenico was silent for a moment, having perfected the art of looking slighted at an inconvenient client request. How could I possibly suggest that they didn't do their job properly? Swiss banks have taken over where Swiss Mercenaries had left off. In Medieval Europe, they could be relied upon to fight to the last man for their client. Their successors, the private banks, are expected to do something similar. Reputation is everything.

Finally, realising that this was something that would not go away, Domenico nodded. "I will pass on your request."

The meeting at an end, I dismissed him and wandered out to the terrace for another view of the lake. A cold wind was blowing from the mountains, carrying the spray from the fountain, and I quickly retreated back into the wonderfully sumptuous surroundings of the Hotel des Bergues. The place where people come to see me.

When the second bank arrived about an hour later, they said almost exactly the same thing as Domenico. So much so, that I called Basel afterwards to check whether the two banks weren't part of the same organisation.

They weren't. They were definitely rivals, and both wanted my business.

I remember lounging in my chair, luxuriating in those surroundings while people in very expensive suits sat on the edges of their seats, trying to win me as a client. Even if the rest of the lobby couldn't hear all that was being said, the meaning was clear. Indiscreet and unadvisable I know, but I loved every moment of it."

6

"I went back to London to wait. Basel was tense, the whole industry was tense. Just about every market commentator had gone quiet, from investment bank strategists to the talking heads on CNBC. Well, the talking heads were still talking, but no longer were they barking that this was 'a once in a lifetime buying opportunity'. They looked increasingly bewildered.

Even the most esoteric parts of the finance world were being widely reported on by the media. Parts that very few people in the industry understood, let alone anyone else.

Until Schwartz Greenberg, the general public had viewed these financial fireworks as something over the horizon, something that had nothing to do with them. But a huge amount of wealth had evaporated in the stockmarket, and a sense of fear was permeating the outside world." Carraway paused, smiling. "I was enjoying it."

"Why?" I asked.

Carraway rolled the beer can between his hands while he considered a reply. "I knew that I had something, and all I had to do was wait. The rest of the world was in a panic, but I felt immune to it all."

"Because you knew something that no one else did?"

Carraway laughed. "I knew nothing. Just like everyone else, I knew basically nothing. But for once in my life I had something that people wanted."

"Getting to see Klein?"

Carraway nodded. "I could sit back and watch the carnage around me, knowing that unlike everyone else, it was actually helping me. Those falling markets had caused Atracor to open the door to me. It wasn't long before Domenico called to say that he'd procured me a meeting. Some of his polish had rubbed off. A hint of irritation, or perhaps it was nerves, snagged on that oily Swiss accent.

He called me late on a Friday, saying that he had organised a meeting for the following Tuesday. I replied that I would have to check my diary, and after a long pause said that I might be able to fit it in.

On the day of the meeting, European stockmarkets looked like they had stabilised, holding ground all morning. But in reality they were waiting for New York to open. It did so with a downward lurch, pulling the rest with it. The only market that wasn't down was Greece, because it was a national holiday and the local market was closed.

The meeting was at four o'clock and ordinarily I would have been stuck in London's afternoon traffic jams, but unlike my previous meeting I didn't have to take a cab. I could walk from my hotel to Atracor's offices.

While the big banks are deserting the City and moving downriver to Canary Wharf, their hedge fund clients have been setting up shop in the opposite direction.

The banks may have their towers of glass, but the hedge fund world is all about anonymous offices in quiet streets. Having started as the preserve of wealthy individuals, London hedge funds located themselves in Mayfair and St James. Their average client now includes pension funds and insurance companies, but if hedge funds want to be taken seriously they still need it to be known that they can afford the right neighbourhood. Only serious money can attract serious money.

The area used to be home to the headquarters of many British multinationals, but they've all moved out over the years, to prove to their shareholders that they were serious about cutting costs. Said shareholders would include many of the hedge funds taking over their old offices.

I followed the address Domenico had given me to a Georgian townhouse just off St James Street. No doubt it has a great view of Green Park, but I didn't have a chance to see that during my visit.

As I expected, there was nothing on the door. Nothing to say that the building was in fact occupied. The sun was close to setting and the street was in deep shadow, but I could see no lights on inside. The ground floor windows were all shuttered.

I buzzed the button alongside the door, conscious of a CCTV camera looking down at me from behind its ring of spikes.

I buzzed a third time, and then a voice crackled "Come up to the first floor."

I pushed on a door that had given no indication that it had unlocked itself. It edged open a crack, and I had to give it another hard push before I could slip inside.

There was a dimly lit entrance hall with no reception area. I would have used the stairs, but they were gated and locked. I took the elevator to the first floor.

A man in his thirties was waiting for me when the elevator arrived. All the doors in the corridor behind him were closed.

He greeted me without giving a name. He had a Euro-American accent and wore a double-breasted suit with a Hermés tie. He led the way to the end of the corridor where he opened a door onto a meeting room with a view of a dark courtyard. The table was inlaid with a beautiful veneer that glowed as he turned on the lights. I sat down opposite him, for a moment totally absorbed by the table as I ran my hand across its exquisite design.

I looked up as he pulled in his chair, banging it against the table. "This is highly unusual," he said, leaning forward. "Our marketing partners handle all new investors."

I nodded. "I understand, and I appreciate your time."

He slid a card across the table. There was no title. I can't remember his surname, but his first name was Petr. He was probably in his late twenties. His hair was carefully gelled into place and his face had a reddish tinge to it, as if he had been standing out in an icy wind.

I put my own card down on the table. He glanced at it, but did not pick it up. "How can I be of assistance, Mr Carraway?"

"I'd like to know more. I'd like to get a feel for how you invest, starting with the philosophy behind it all."

Petr smiled. "As Banque Privé have no doubt already told you, they conduct all due diligence on your behalf. Everything you need to know, they know already." In other words, don't waste my time.

"And as *you* will know, I don't have a longstanding relationship with Banque Privé. They appear to be good at what they do, but they're not going to be managing my three hundred million francs. You are. No doubt you'll appreciate that I'd like to know more about the underlying process before I commit that kind of money."

Petr sat back in the chair, folding his arms. "Mr Carraway, we are not a bunch of day-traders. Do you seriously think that Atracor could have done so well, for so long, if we were? Everyone thinks that we have a machine into which we feed data at one end, while it spits trades out the other. The reality couldn't be more different."

"But you're a quant-based fund, right?"

"Do you know anything about quantitative investing?"

"A little."

"At the very least, you would know that it's not a case of having a single magic formula that works day in, day out while you sit back and watch the money roll in." Petr waved his hand around the room. "Forget the machines. Atracor's success is based on a huge, ongoing investment in human capital. This is a large organisation of very talented and highly intelligent people."

"And one person in particular."

Petr sighed, rubbing his forehead. "The common misconception. If you'd let Banque Privé brief you fully, you would know that Atracor is not about a single genius and his algorithms."

"But Klein is the driving force behind it, right?"

"Dr Klein founded Atracor Capital almost forty years ago, in his spare room. After a highly successful track record over four decades, Atracor has grown into something far greater than that. As I've just said, we have many highly intelligent, highly qualified people here. The sense of collaboration is unique."

"So who is best able to explain your process to me?"

"Your contact at Banque Privé."

"Who didn't tell me much at all."

"Perhaps you should give him more time."

The meeting was going nowhere. I decided to cut to the chase. "I would like to see him."

"Who?"

"Klein. Dr Klein."

Petr shook his head. "That is not something we offer to new clients."

"But this is a very large investment."

"As I said, we do not offer it to new clients."

"How long would I have to wait until I saw him?"

Petr smiled. "Most of our clients have been with us for a very long time, many of them since inception. That's the way we like it. That's why we don't have to go out and appeal to new clients."

I was about to speak, but he waved me to silence. "Atracor is by far the longest running hedge fund there is. How has that been achieved? Quite simply because Dr Klein's philosophy has always been about the long term. You couldn't invest and expect to see him in a week. Dr Klein thinks in terms of years, not months, not weeks. That is why he has done better than anyone."

"*He*? I thought it wasn't just about him."

Petr's lips tightened. "Dr Klein is our founder and our majority owner. His investment philosophy built Atracor."

"So how about running me through it?"

As I said, the investment process is extremely complex. It is not something that we can sit here and summarise in ten minutes."

"I have time."

Petr shook his head. "The entire market is trying to replicate what we're doing. Why on earth would we give anyone even an inkling of the secret of our success?"

"I'm not just anyone. I'm considering a three hundred million franc investment."

Petr looked unimpressed. "As Banque Privé would have told you, we are capacity constrained. There is very little new money that we can take, if at all. So the size of your potential investment matters very little to us. In fact, the bigger it is, the less we want it."

"But the fact that you're seeing me suggests that you do want it. You need it."

I expected him to react, but he didn't flinch. "Mr Carraway, we don't need anything, or anyone. You should simply thank Banque Privé for intervening on your behalf. And you should listen to what they have to say."

"As I said, they told me nothing."

"They did tell you that there really isn't much point coming to see us. Because there's nothing to say. Either you like our returns and we accept you as a client, or we part ways. It's really that simple."

"You expect every new client to accept everything on blind faith?

"Not at all. Our returns are plain to see."

"In that case, why don't we take a look at them?"

Petr opened a folder and took out a sheet of paper, sliding it across the table. It was the same document that Banque Privé had shown me. Monthly returns for the last five years, preceded by annual returns going right back to the inception of the fund. In this case, the table had been updated for February. That had been an awful month for the markets, but Atracor was up. Not by much, but still up in a market where just about every stock and every asset class was falling.

"Let's talk about February," I said.

"What of it?"

"How did you manage to be in positive territory? There's been nowhere to hide. Everyone's been taking hits."

"Clearly not *everyone*," said Petr dryly.

"But I would have thought-"

"If you knew anything about investing, you would know that you can make just as much money from a falling market as a rising one."

"Where did your best performance come from? Was it specific stocks, or industries, or-"

"It was simply from a superior investment process, Mr Carraway."

"I need more than that."

Petr looked out the window at the dark courtyard. "For investors who require transparency, Atracor is not the right investment. That should be clear from the outset."

"I just want some comfort, that's all."

He looked back at me as if I had just said the most ridiculous thing. "We're hiding nothing. We're upfront about that. If you don't like it, go elsewhere. It's that simple." He stood up. "Thanks for stopping by."

I picked up the sheet of paper, but he held out his hand. "I'll be keeping that, thank you."

I followed him to the elevator and we waited in silence while it ascended. The doors slid soundlessly open and he leaned in and pressed the button for the ground floor. I stepped in, the doors closing behind me before I could turn around."

Carraway began coughing as black smoke blew across the deck. The roof of a sampan came past, puttering loudly. He waited until it was gone, covering his mouth and nose. The tide had already risen some way up the quayside, and the other boats were much closer as they shuttled back and forth.

"Those damn two-stroke engines," said Jongstra as he watched the sampan pass by.

Carraway smiled. "The Mekong Delta isn't exactly an idyllic retreat."

"You got that right," said Valassis. "All that racket. And the hassle. Everyone hassling you for a dime."

"Where are you going next?" I asked.

"Up the coast."

"Anywhere in particular?"

Valassis shrugged, glancing at his watch. "Wherever I feel like. Maybe Nha Trang. I hear there are good beaches."

"You're a surfer?"

"Hell no. I fish."

"You've been fishing the Mekong?"

He nodded. "Have you heard of Mekong Catfish? They're huge."

"You don't want to eat anything out of this river," said Jongstra. "The Mekong runs through most of Southeast Asia's cities. It's a sewer."

"Who said anything about eating it?" Valassis scanned the crowd on the quayside, evidently looking to see if Lan was on her way back. There was no sign of her. After a few moments he sat back down, watching Carraway while relighting his cigar. "Why don't you tell us what you're doing in Vietnam?"

Carraway shrugged. "Taking a break. Just like everyone else."

"You've finished the investigation?"

"As I said, it wasn't-"

"Whatever the hell you want to call it. You've finished?"

Carraway nodded.

"So what did you find?"

Carraway smiled. "If I told you that now, I wouldn't have a story. You wanted a story, didn't you?"

Valassis took a draw on the cigar, releasing its smoke into the slanting sunlight. "Pick up the pace. This boat is leaving in half an hour."

"I was more or less back where I had started, scratching around for whatever leads I could find. I met up with Glenn for another round of drinks. The last time I had seen him, he had droned on about how little free time he had. But he seemed to have time for drinks, with me of all people, and I'd come to the conclusion that I didn't like him at all.

He wasn't nearly as cocky this time. In fact, his mood was black. He didn't care what they put in the Martinis. The bar was emptier. He had complained how full it was the time before, but now he kept looking around, as if he was wondering where everyone had gone.

We were only just into our first round of drinks when he let slip that his team had suffered some big losses on their derivatives trades. Trusted models that used to work weren't working at all. Everything was coming unstuck. He told me that he arrived at work every morning expecting to be smashed in the face.

"What do you mean?" I said.

"We're taking hits left, right and centre. It's just one thing after another. The data's all fucked. You can't rely on anything anymore."

"What do you mean?"

"The ratings agencies have fucked up royally. They took lead and called it gold, assigning Triple-A ratings to mortgage debt that's plain junk. That stuff is now out in the market, poisoning everything. When people lose faith in ratings, what do you have to go on? You can't rate every bond yourself."

"What exactly did the agencies do wrong?"

"They thought they were so fucking clever. Subprime mortgages didn't exist at all until a few years ago. There was no historical data for them to build their models, but there was huge demand in the market so what did they do? They synthesised theoretical data, crunched it through their models and presto! Everything was magically assigned a rating when there was no fucking way you could take an opinion on it at all."

"But it's mortgage debt. If it defaults, the house is sold and in the fullness of time you get repaid."

"Not in the real world. As it turns out, the price of that house was inflated by a bubble that's now burst. And that mortgage debt is everywhere. It's been repackaged and sold on so many times, that it's like Chlamydia in Freshers' week. It's everywhere.

We weren't stupid enough to hold any of that crap, but it still hasn't helped us. The market has completely seized up. No bank can afford to take the loss by selling any of it." He paused, finishing the last of his Martini in one swallow. "That was bad enough, then Schwartz Greenberg goes bust and now they're trying to unwind billions of dollars of trades when there isn't enough liquidity. They're just dumping it in the market regardless."

"Was the bank really worth just a dollar when it was sold?"

Glenn waved his empty glass at the bartender. "Nobody has a fucking clue what it's worth. If you want a price, you need a buyer for every seller, but if there's all sellers and no buyers, there's no fucking market. There's no price."

"So why did the sale happen?"

"Because the Fed didn't want Schwartz to go bust. With all the interconnections between Schwartz Greenberg and the other banks, *no one* wanted Schwartz to go bust. It would have spread like a heart attack through the system."

"So they were bailed out?"

He shook his head. "Schwartz wasn't bailed out. The Fed didn't want the financial system to seize up, but they also didn't want to create moral hazard. That means giving people the message that they will be rescued no matter what.

But they had to lance the boil. So they took Schwartz Greenberg into the street and shot it in front of everyone. At one dollar per share, that's effectively what they did to Schwartz's shareholders." Glenn gave a grim smile. "Like what the French said when the British executed an admiral who had had failed to win a battle against them. 'Pour encourager les autres.'"

"Do you think it's solved the problem?"

"Jesus, how would I know? I'm just trying to stay afloat, day by day."

"But do you think there's a risk that the whole banking system could go bankrupt? Another Great Depression, with a queue outside every bank, everyone in a panic to withdraw their money?"

Glenn shook his head. "The chances of that are zero. The Fed drew a line in the sand with Schwartz Greenberg, and the line held."

"So you're not worried?"

"Where the hell do you think all my hair has gone? Of course I'm worried. I'm fucking worried. To stay alive in this game, you've got to be permanently worried."

That second evening of drinks with Glenn did throw up something useful. He reminded me of an ex-colleague who had become a hedge fund manager, and then moved on to the marketing side. For all its secrecy, the hedge fund world is actually a village. It's small and gossipy, and everyone knows pretty much everyone. Or they think they do.

The guy's name is Jeremy. I gave him a call. He remembered me. Incredibly, he was available to meet at short notice.

Just as implausibly, the restaurant he suggested was half empty. It's a trendy Japanese place just off Piccadilly, where the staff keep a respectful distance.

I had no idea how he would be. When we had worked together he was the archetypical political animal, superficially friendly to all, impossible to read. I never counted him as much more than a colleague.

He stopped at a table as he came in, chatting to the people there for a few moments. Like Glenn, he had put on a lot of weight but at least he still had his hair, looking like it was blow-dried. In spite of what was going on in the markets he seemed relaxed, almost jovial. He shook my hand as though we were old friends, holding it for a little longer than was necessary. He asked what I was doing with my life, as if he was genuinely interested.

We made the obligatory small-talk for a few minutes and then, after we had placed our orders, I cut to the chase.

Jeremy's eyes were suddenly alive with interest. "Is he under investigation? Are you investigating Klein?"

"Not exactly. I'm just trying to find out more. He's become so influential that the people in Basel can't ignore him any more."

"They're afraid of him?"

"You could say that."

Jeremy nodded, reaching for his glass. "They should be. Klein is the market, and the market is what makes the world go round. They can't stop it, just like you can't stop nature." He took a sip of water and put the glass down. "You asked me to lunch because you think I know something about Klein?"

"Or Atracor. Anything you've heard in the market would be helpful."

"Am I your first port of call?"

I shook my head. "I've already tried to see Klein. I went to Atracor Capital a few days ago."

"And?"

"I got nothing."

Jeremy smiled, shaking his head at my naïveté. "Didn't someone tell you that he refuses to see anyone? He doesn't even meet investors."

"Do you have any idea why?"

Jeremy shrugged, taking another sip of water. "No doubt he has a ton of reasons. But from a marketing point of view it's obvious."

"How so?"

"Being so secretive, so unavailable, so completely hidden, gives him an 'Oz' allure. Investors love it, like bees around honey."

"Is there anyone else at Atracor who might speak to me?"

Jeremy shook his head. "Klein prizes loyalty above everything. His employees have never worked anywhere else. He gets them straight out of college. They are handpicked by him, and trained by him. Who else have you asked?"

"His feeder funds. I posed as an investor."

"I presume you've already realised that's a waste of time. Klein forbids the feeder funds from even listing his name in any of their prospectuses."

"Why?"

"Because he's not regulated. It's like prostitution, right? In itself it's not illegal, but to solicit is. The way the rules work, Klein can pretty much do whatever he likes, as long as he's not soliciting business from anyone."

"But if he's never listed in the prospectuses, how do clients know to invest?"

"Word of mouth. Everyone knows which are the Klein feeder funds. In any case, nobody ever reads prospectuses. If they did, they probably wouldn't invest a penny. They go on what the private banks tell them."

"Which is what people like you tell the private banks."

Jeremy smiled. "It may come as a surprise to you, but we're more professional than that. At the end of the day, as a hedge fund we have to sing for our supper. If our performance is crap, we're out. But the private banks are all about image and prestige. Your average private banker doesn't do anything other than schmooze. He invariably has some minor aristocratic title, which puts a veneer of respectability on the whole thing. It harks back to an age when everything was grander and bankers were gentlemen. Private banking clients love it. They suck it up." Jeremy stopped as our sashimi arrived.

"And now you come to me," he said after the waitress had disappeared.

I nodded.

Jeremy picked up a sliver of tuna with his chopsticks and held it aloft. "Let me ask you a question. Why should I tell you anything?"

"It's just a chat."

"But you want more than that. It's not a chat if I tell you something you want to know." He slipped the tuna into his mouth and seemed to swallow it without chewing. "I mean, why does anyone disclose anything? So they can get something in return."

"We used to work together, and I thought-"

He laughed, putting down his chopsticks. "We haven't seen each other for years, and suddenly I get a call out of the blue. It's not as if we ever had lunch when we worked together."

I didn't reply, picking out a piece of salmon with my chopsticks.

"It's because you want something. It's not because we worked together, or were even friends. It's because you want something."

I put the salmon back down. "You want me to pay you?"

He laughed again, reaching for his water. "Hey, I'm just fucking with you. You're buying me lunch anyway, aren't you? And what I know of Klein isn't worth more than this lunch." He glanced at his glass of water. "Wine not included."

"I wasn't expecting you to know anything specific. I was just looking for some background. Some colour."

"Colour? On Klein?"

I nodded.

"Have you ever considered that what he's doing is the pits?"

"What do you mean?"

"Being a hedge fund manager is just about the worst job there is. You've always got to stay ahead of the best and the brightest that the world has to offer." By now Jeremy had exhausted all the tuna on his plate, and he poked around the rest of the sashimi, pushing the squid to one side. "That's why I'm in marketing. I couldn't make it as a fund manager. But at least I realised and got out in time."

He finally selected a piece of mackerel and slipped it into his mouth. "Funny how salmon used to be more expensive than mackerel. But these days they farm so much damn salmon that it's cheap as chips, while mackerel is overfished and becomes a rarity. I never used to even think of eating mackerel, but now that it's expensive I'm growing to like it." He swallowed, and took a sip of water. "Sure, I don't get paid as well as the fund managers, but I'm still paid way better than any other industry there is. And I still have a job at the end of the day.

If a fund manager fucks up, he's out. For good. In this industry no one will hire you again. And a fuck-up in this industry isn't like a fuck-up anywhere else. You don't actually have to do anything wrong. You can still be doing great, but if the average manager is doing better than you, you've fucked up.

It didn't take me long to realise that all I had to do was attach myself to a successful manager and sell his fund. He's the cavalry, right? He leads the charge, and gets all the glory. Without him, we wouldn't win the battle. But a shit-load of them don't ever make it to the other end.

As for me, I'm at the back, watching to see who's about to be hit by a cannon ball, and who's going to make it all the way through." Jeremy slipped another piece of mackerel into his mouth and sat back in his chair, chewing.

"If you've marketed a great fund, some of that lustre rubs off on you even though, let's face it, a monkey could market a successful fund. The best marketers aren't people like me. They're the ones who have to market third and fourth quartile funds. But those poor bastards are destined to sink into obscurity." Jeremy smiled, scooping a final piece of mackerel into his mouth. "You remember that old saying? 'Success has many fathers, but failure is an orphan'."

He sat back in his chair, looking pleased with himself. As he did so, something caught his eye and he stood up and walked across the restaurant. A couple of diners had just sat down at a table near the window, the first new customers since we had arrived. He shook hands with them and stood chatting for a few moments before he returned.

"It never stops," he said as he sat down. "Bunch of fucking pricks, but hey. That's my job."

"Do you know anything specific to Klein?" I said.

Jeremy leaned forward, putting both elbows on the table. "You want to know about Klein? I'll sum it up for you. Klein is everything that we're trying to do. We've got a shitload of brains and experience and capital and energy, and we're not there yet. What does that tell you about Klein?"

I shrugged. "Kind of what I already knew."

"Like I said, what I know isn't worth more than this lunch." Jeremy pushed his plate away. All that remained were salmon and squid pieces.

"But surely you must be curious. Haven't you tried to second-guess how he's doing it?"

Jeremy shrugged. "No doubt you've heard of Klein's fabled algorithms."

"What about them?"

"It explains everything. Nobody can perform as consistently as Atracor has. It's something only a computer could achieve."

"A bunch of algorithms are not more intelligent than a human being."

Jeremy shook his head. "You've never been a fund manager. You've got to do the exact opposite of what every human being would do. You've got to ignore the crowd behaviour that drives markets, that drives our instinct to follow after, forever a step behind."

"But no algorithm is perfect. They eventually run their course. Why do his keep working?"

"Because no one else has figured them out. The simple fact that Klein is still churning out superior returns, month in month out, tells you that no one else has figured them out. Which is precisely why he's so secretive. The moment someone works out the formula to his secret sauce, it's all over. The whole thing evaporates overnight."

Valassis put down his beer with a loud chink. "What are you saying?"

"What about?" said Carraway.

"What are you saying? The clock is ticking for Klein? That one day it'll all come crashing down? Is that what you're saying?"

Carraway sat watching him for a few moments. "Do you have an interest in this? Do you know Klein?"

"I asked the question. Where exactly are you going with this? And what's this crap about coming here for a break? What are you really doing in Vietnam?"

Carraway shrugged. "A break is a break."

Valassis shook his head. "Everyone knows that Emerging Markets are a Klein favourite. He was there in the late nineties, when no one else wanted to touch them. And when everybody followed behind, he was already moving on from the more established markets like China and Russia, to places like Vietnam. Just look how the market here took off as a result. What do you want to do, prosecute him for being ahead of the game?"

"You seem to know a lot about him. What exactly-"

"I asked the question. You want to prosecute him for being ahead of the game?"

Carraway shook his head. "I've never said anything about prosecuting Klein."

"But you've followed him here."

"I'm done with all that. The story I'm telling happened almost two years ago. It's over and done with, and I came here for a break. How about answering my question. What do *you* know about Klein?"

Valassis looked across the river, taking a draw on his cigar. "I know the markets, I know of him."

"How much do you know?"

"Maybe more than you. Finish your story, and we'll see."

7

Valassis spotted someone on the quayside and whistled.

We all turned to look. Lan was walking back to the boat.

"Where are they?" shouted Valassis.

She replied that they were on their way. We watched as she walked through the crowd towards us. She moved swiftly, but without any evident effort in the heat of the afternoon. The yacht had risen some way up the quayside since she had left, and she barely broke her step as she came aboard.

"Get us something to eat, will you?"

She nodded and disappeared into the cabin.

Valassis turned to Carraway, flicking ash from his cigar over the side of the yacht. "What happened next?"

"Basel arranged for me to meet a competitor of Klein's. Atracor were head and shoulders above everyone, but this man was about as close a second as you could find. He had been in the business almost as long as Klein, and his returns were good. In fact you would have said they were great, had Klein not existed."

"That's the trouble with skill," I said. "It's all relative."

"On the contrary," said Jongstra, "That's the *good* thing about it. In the world of the blind, the one-eyed man is king." He smiled. "That's why we're all here, right?"

"Please explain," I said.

"It's like colonialism all over again. We can be far bigger here than we would ever be back home. Only this time round we don't have to risk getting malaria in the process."

"And what are you trying to be here?" said Valassis.

"I should be retired by now," said Jongstra, "but things haven't gone as planned. But I've got something which, if it works out, should set me up nicely."

"Care to share it with us?" I asked.

"Activated carbon. It's going to be a huge growth market. Public health standards for tap water are being upgraded all over the world, and the best filters are made from activated carbon. For that the best raw material is eucalyptus, and Vietnam has loads of it."

"But eucalyptus is Australian."

"Yes, but it will grow just about anywhere. During the war, the forests in this country were wiped out by Napalm and Agent Orange. They needed something that could grow quickly in the poor tropical soils, and eucalyptus is perfect." He glanced at his watch. "Anyway, enough of that. We should let Carraway finish his story before our host sets sail."

Carraway smiled in response. "Your venture sounds like a good opportunity. Wouldn't you all rather hear about that, than what I have to say? It won't be nearly as rewarding."

"We've listened this far," I said. "You might as well finish it."

He smiled again. "As any fund manager would tell you, always disregard sunk costs."

"The man's name is Leon Rom. I was surprised that he'd agreed to see me. I guess Basel have influence, unless of course he had some other agenda.

We met for lunch at a restaurant of his choice. The place is a favourite for hedge fund managers, or hedgies as they're called. The term sounds kind of warm and cuddly, doesn't it? Leon Rom is anything but.

I had to wait some time before he finally arrived. All the staff knew him, but he wasn't friendly with them. They were very efficient and took great care to leave us undisturbed.

Rom was of average height, average stature, with an average suit, in fact there wasn't anything to tell you that this man was worth billions. He moved slowly and had a pinched look across his face. Perhaps it was all those hidden billions weighing on him.

I ordered another San Pellegrino, as I had already drunk most of the bottle they had put on the table. When the waitress left I explained why I was there, without giving away too much detail. Rom sat in silence for a while after I had finished, with one eye on the Blackberry he had placed on the table in front of him.

"Where exactly is this leading?" he said at last.

"It would help us if you could tell me what you know about Klein."

"Nobody knows anything about Klein."

"But you must have an opinion."

Rom picked up his Blackberry and thumbed the wheel. After a few moments, he looked up. "You want an opinion? You don't know the facts, and you think an opinion will suffice?" He sounded like he was getting ready to pass judgement, but the waitress reappeared with another bottle of San Pellegrino and we watched in silence while she poured the water. Rom reached for his glass and took a sip, keeping an eye on the waitress as she walked away.

I started over. "We are completely in the dark about Klein, and we think that you can help. Someone in your position should be able to make some observations."

Rom picked up his Blackberry as it pinged and spent some time reading the message. Finally, he looked up at me. "Everyone talks about Atracor's fabulous track record, but nobody ever thinks to ask one very important question."

"Which is?"

"You mean you don't know?"

"We're considering a number of things."

"Like what?"

"His use of information on order flows from market makers. His use of quote stuffing to slow down exchanges-"

"You don't have a fucking clue. I'm talking debt. An investment manager's return is meaningless without knowing how much debt lies behind it." Rom put his glass down. "Debt is at the heart of every successful hedge fund strategy. But attaining what Klein has achieved requires an inordinate amount of it."

"Why do you say that?"

"When you're the size that Klein is, you can't generate the kind of returns that he does. You're too damn big."

"You're saying he can get there using debt?"

Rom nodded. "With enough debt, anyone can generate the most spectacular returns from the dowdiest of investments. The one case where you can make a silk purse out of a sow's ear. Not the first time this industry has proved the Bible wrong." He picked up his Blackberry again and slowly buffed the screen with his sleeve. "Take an example. Klein produces a thirty percent return in an average year and investors say 'Wow, the man's a genius'. Bullshit. All he's done is leverage up thirty times and invest in something that produces a return just one percent above the cost of his debt. Presto, a thirty percent return. A chimpanzee could do that."

Rom raised his hand and a waitress came over. She took our orders and left again.

"The chimp looks like a genius, but it's creating an unsustainable position. Klein cannot carry on like that forever. Everyone is doing the same thing, and spreads have tightened. Klein's returns should be fading, but they're not.

It would follow that he's taking on even greater levels of debt. If he fucks up- and he *will* fuck up, everyone will be in deep shit as that mountain of debt comes crashing down. Tell me, are you looking into that?"

I shrugged as if I couldn't possibly comment. In reality I didn't know the answer.

Fortunately his Blackberry pinged again and he read the message, frowning. He took another sip of water as if he needed to wash down the news.

By then I'd thought of something to say. I asked him who on earth would lend Klein that much money, on such good terms? It wouldn't make sense, even to the largest banks.

Rom laughed. "Bankers are falling over themselves to extend Klein credit."

"But why?"

"The magic of leverage works for them just as it works for him. The banks have become debt junkies just like their favourite client. Klein offers the prospect of huge volumes, in addition to the arrangement fees and brokerage fees. Not to mention the fact that Klein makes markets. For that fact alone, they all want to get involved with him."

"Who are his main lenders?"

Rom shrugged. "How should I know? That's something you people should be targeting. That's if you actually do anything in Basel." He sat watching me, as though I had proved all his suppositions about my species.

"You think it's all explained by debt?" I asked.

"Of course not."

"Then what else?"

"When you talk to anyone about Klein's performance, what is the rote answer?"

"His algorithms."

Rom nodded, taking another sip of water. "Klein's fabled algorithms. Ask yourself a question. This is the most competitive industry there is. It attracts the most intelligent and driven people the world has to offer. How come no one else has managed to match Klein's returns?"

Without waiting for a reply, he continued. "If a certain strategy succeeds, there will always be copy-cats following close behind. It's not as if they've gone out and stolen the algorithm, it's simply the law of evolution. The most successful strategies will succeed, while the less successful will fail.

Most algorithms are designed to identify small, short-term anomalies in securities prices by crunching reams of data. But computer processing has become so cheap that just about anybody can buy as much of it as they like. What does that mean?" Rom smiled as he slowly turned the glass in his hand, inspecting the rim. "Mathematical genius is dead. Any Joe Schmo can crunch billions of bits of data, and keep on crunching, until he ends up with pretty much the same algorithms that Klein is using. At that moment, the game is up." Rom took a final swallow of water, pursing his lips as though it were bitter. "But no one has caught up with Klein in forty years, so what does that tell you?"

At that moment the waitress returned, placing a plate of pasta in front of Rom and a salad in front of me. Rom picked up a fork and poked around the linguine, isolating a clam shell and scooping out its meat. I followed his lead, taking a mouthful of salad. We sat munching on our respective dishes in silence. I felt like the whole restaurant was watching us.

"So he's not using algorithms," I said.

Rom nodded. "Klein's technique is not quant based at all. All that spiel about algorithms is a lie."

"Why would he do that?"

Rom scooped the meat out of another clam shell and slowly chewed on it while he watched the Blackberry in front of him. "In an industry obsessed with secrecy, Klein takes it to a whole new level. Secrecy is the very essence of Atracor. If you're a client, you don't question anything. Anyone who has the temerity to ask, gets told 'If you don't like what we do, take your money back.' Atracor justifies its obsession for secrecy by the need to protect those magic formulas." Rom paused, looking around the restaurant. "But if the algorithms don't exist, what's really driving that requirement for secrecy?"

I shrugged. "It could be one of many things."

"But what's the most obvious? You should know this. What is the single biggest reason why people stash their money in Switzerland?"

"Tax?"

"Exactly. Tax evasion." Rom isolated another clam shell with his fork, but it was closed and he pushed it to the side of the plate. "What you should be asking is whether all those billions that Klein manages have ever been declared. Has a penny of it ever shown up on a tax return?"

"That's not our remit. We wouldn't-"

"Atracor wouldn't be the first hedge fund to do it. Everybody knows that Long Term Capital were busy avoiding tax, conjuring up elaborate schemes to throw the IRS off the scent." Rom looked up as the waitress approached, his hand held protectively over his Blackberry. She refilled our glasses and disappeared again. "What's the second reason why people hide their money in Switzerland?"

"Client service?" I said.

"Don't give me that crap. It's money laundering. Well, it was. The OECD has been cracking down on offshore locations for some time now, so that it's almost impossible to launder anything of any size. People will pay forty to fifty percent to get it done." He looked up at me. "You asked where Klein gets his returns. Maybe you haven't been looking in the right places."

"Those are pretty big allegations. Do you have any proof?"

"They're observations. But where there's smoke, there's fire. It's time the authorities looked through that smokescreen, and determined the cause of the blaze down below." Rom picked out another clam and chewed on it, washing it down with San Pellegrino. "And that brings me onto my final observation. "How have Klein's returns been so stable? He's only had five down months in the last ten years. How the hell has he managed that?"

"I've heard that he's not always in the market. He's in and out when he pleases."

"How do you think a fund of that size finds the liquidity to do it? In any case no one else has managed to time the market that well, over such a long period."

"That's what I'm here to find out."

Rom spat a piece of shell onto the plate and plucked out another clam. "It's very simple. The athlete who keeps winning every race isn't playing by the rules. He's on a performance enhancing drug."

"Like what?"

"Inside information."

"But that would have to be on a massive scale. How could Klein possibly-"

"It's easily done. You've heard of expert networks?"

I shook my head.

"They recruit employees of public companies, getting them to moonlight as 'consultants'. They operate under the guise of providing 'industry insight' but the real aim is to get them to pass on non-public information to hedge funds and other clients."

"That happens?"

"It happens all the time. There's a fine line between providing insight versus divulging market sensitive information. It could be as simple as the number of people going into a particular retailer. It could be more advanced, like a geologist from Exxon revealing the results of their seismic surveys. Not necessarily market sensitive information, until he lets slip that they've made a major new find.

Even the legit consultancies are guilty. The great and good McKinseys and Bains call it 'strategic consulting', but at heart they trade information. Companies hire management consultants to ensure that they don't fall behind their competitors. But in doing so, they become engaged in a trade. In return for parting with their own secrets, they gain access to their rivals' secrets which the consultants dress up as 'industry best practice'.

A management consultancy is essentially a little Switzerland. A neutral party that enables an information flow between arch rivals, such that the partners in those firms are at the hub of a massive amount of information. Each of them will pull down a couple of million a year, but it's peanuts compared to what they can get if they pass on that information to the likes of Klein."

"I take it Klein isn't the only one tapping onto it?"

"Klein isn't tapping into it. He's opened a vein. He can recruit people directly from the companies themselves. Thanks to social networking sites and job-search sites, he can scan thousands of résumés just like any legitimate recruiter. It's very easy to conduct a search to find out who works where.

Klein doesn't even need groundbreaking information. He just needs to know in which direction it will move the price, even by a tiny bit. That's all." Rom sat back in his seat, looking at me. "That leaves me having to compete on an uneven playing field. People like Klein are on financial steroids, and they're getting away with it. Someone is not doing their job. Someone is asleep at the wheel."

"Who would that be?" I asked.

"All you regulators. The SEC, the FSA, you people in Basel. You know what the problem is? Your organisations are wall-to-wall with lawyers. You may understand securities law back to front, but you know fuck-all about how the financial world works in practice." Rom pushed his plate away. All the clams had been picked out, leaving the pasta behind."

"Let me get something clear," said Valassis. "Those are serious allegations. You followed them up?"

Carraway shook his head. "I haven't finished the story."

"Just what kind of an investigation is this anyway? All you're going on is the view of a competitor who Klein has beaten hands-down. Why else do you think he was prepared to speak to you? It was just to get at Klein."

Carraway shrugged. "Rom made some observations. Nothing more."

"Tell me something," said Valassis, leaning forward in his seat. "Just what exactly have you done with this information?"

I compiled a report, and sent it to Basel."

"You're telling us something that hasn't been publicised yet?"

"Who said anything about it being publicised?"

"Then what have they done with it?"

"I have no idea."

We looked up as Lan appeared out of the cabin with a platter of spring rolls. She put them down on the table and collected the empty beer cans before returning back down below.

Valassis caught my eye as I watched her stepping back into the cabin. "The women in this part of the world like to stay in the shade. They prize a pale complexion." He reached forward, taking a spring roll and dunking it into the dipping sauce in the centre of the platter. "It's associated with beauty," he said, munching on the roll. "Help yourselves."

We all followed his example, reaching forward at once. Carraway withdrew, letting me and Jongstra take first before he selected a spring roll for himself. They weren't deep-fried, but fresh, delicately wrapped in rice paper.

"It's got lettuce," said Jongstra, inspecting the one he had taken.

Valassis looked at him. "So?"

"Is it okay to eat?"

"Of course it's okay to eat. This is my yacht." He turned to Carraway. "Get on with your story."

"I reported back to Basel, but got little reaction. I don't know if it was something they were expecting, or if they doubted Rom's credibility.

But they made it clear that they wanted me to come up with more. Stockmarkets were still under pressure, even though the trading volume in the major exchanges wasn't large at all. It was as if the main impetus was coming from somewhere else, like those dark pools which I talked about earlier.

The takeover of Schwartz Greenberg hadn't been any help to the banks. Their stock prices were sinking daily. The regulators were convinced that hedge funds like Atracor were responsible, aggressively shorting banks knowing that it was a one-way street for them, just like it had been with Schwartz. The regulators' response was to ban all short-selling of financial stocks, but it did little to halt the slide.

Everyone seemed bewildered, gripped by a creeping anxiety. There was quite simply nowhere to hide. Not even deposits were safe anymore, because most of the banks were teetering. Not even cash under your mattress was safe, because inflation was starting to rear up, eating away at it.

In the midst of that, another round of drinks with Glenn paid off. He got me a meeting which was very different from the others, with someone who had actually worked for Klein. Until then, all I was getting was the view of people from the outside. But here was someone from the inside, who was prepared to talk. Basel were impressed, because nobody who had worked for Atracor had ever spoken about it in all the years the firm had been in operation.

His name is André. I met him at his home. I expected him to want to meet somewhere else, but he said to come round one evening after work.

The address was in Hampstead, one of the nicest parts of London. It was a beautiful house just a few yards from the Heath. I guessed that he was in his mid thirties, so he had done well to afford that kind of house.

When I arrived, he looked terrible. He offered me a beer and sat with a glass of water.

"So you want to know about Klein," he said. There was a trace of a French accent beneath the American.

I nodded.

"Why?"

I gave him the usual spiel, that it wasn't an investigation, just an enquiry. Atracor had become so large that we quite simply had to know more about it.

He looked at the glass of water for a few moments, slowly turning it in his hands. "If you want to know about Klein, you need to know all of it."

"All of what?" I asked.

"Look at me. What do you see?"

I shook my head. "What do you mean?"

"Do I look like I'm in reasonable shape to you?"

"Well, I really don't-"

"I'm in terrible shape. My hair's been falling out for years. That's why I shave it, because there's hardly anything left. I keep getting ulcers and cold sores. I'm always on antibiotics. And it's not like I've done anything to deserve it. When I was a student, eating crap and partying all the time, I didn't get any of this. I haven't been whoring around, and I haven't been backpacking through Asia. All I've been doing is going to the office every day. And yet I keep getting infections, because my immune system is so low."

"I'm sorry to hear that," I said.

"It's what comes from ten years in the industry. It's my eleventh anniversary next month. And just look at me."

"You've got a nice place," I said.

He gave a wry smile, looking around the room. "But not nice enough. It could be better. It could always be better. That's why I'm still at it, even though I'm killing myself." He looked back at me. "I know what you're thinking. You're wondering what the hell this has to do with Klein."

I nodded.

"You need something from me. I need to get something off my chest. We can meet halfway. In any case, you've got to understand the industry."

"What about it?"

"At its most base, it feeds two emotions. Fear and greed. People go into this industry because they are greedy. Over time, that greed feeds fear."

"Fear of what?"

"Fear of not having enough." André tipped back his head and took a long swallow of water. "You become terrified of losing not only what you have, but what you could have. I don't think I've ever been particularly greedy, but I know that I've become damn well afraid." He finished the water, and put the glass down.

"It's not the fear of absolute loss, but relative loss. The fear of having less than the people around you. It's unbearable. You'll do anything to prevent that, and they've got you hooked."

"*They?*"

"The system."

"You're saying that it's all been planned this way?"

He shook his head. "Not at all. Nobody could have planned it so well. We bring it on ourselves. That's the worst of it. As long as we stay in the game, we've got no one to blame but ourselves." He looked down. "Well I'm sick of it. I'm spitting out the hook. I'm done."

I heard footsteps at the far end of the room. I looked up. A woman was standing there, arms folded. She wore a black cocktail dress and looked like she was about to go out.

"Done with what?" she said. She sounded American.

"This is my wife," he said without looking up. "Sorry, I've forgotten your name."

"Carraway," I said to the woman. "Chris Carraway."

"What are you done with?" she said, her eyes fixed on her husband.

"I'm quitting the fund," he said, looking at me.

She stepped into the middle of the room. "You've had another offer?"

He shook his head. "No, I'm quitting. Simple as that."

"Quitting to do what?"

He didn't reply.

"Quitting to do *what*?" she repeated.

"Nothing." He looked up at her. "Right now, nothing."

She took a step closer. "What do you mean, *nothing*?"

"I'm out of it. For once in my life, I'm going to do something that I actually enjoy."

"What's that?"

He shrugged. "I guess I'll find out."

"And at what point were you going to discuss this with me?"

"Now, I guess."

"And who is this?" She looked at me. "Who the hell is he?"

"I should go," I said, putting the beer down.

André put up his hand. "It's fine." He looked up at his wife. "We're fine with what we have. We don't need any more."

"*Really*? Things didn't seem so fine last week, when you told me how much your portfolio had lost. What makes everything so hunky-dory today?"

"In the greater scheme of things, we are fine. I can go on to do something else."

She shook her head. "And what exactly is that going to be?"

He shrugged. "I'll think of something."

"And what do we do in the meantime? The renovations haven't even started. How are we going to pay for them if you don't have a job?"

"The house is fine the way it is. We've just bought our holiday home, and both are pretty much paid for. What more could you want?"

"It's not on the water."

He frowned. "What do you mean?"

"It's two blocks from the water."

"So what?"

"Is that the best we're going to get? I don't want a vacation home that's not on the water. I said you should never leave Atracor. I told you that, but you wouldn't listen. Look at you now, you're a mess."

"I'd better go," I said, standing up.

This time André didn't stop me. He showed me to the door, opening it to reveal reflections of the streetlights in the asphalt outside. It was a typical London rain, not heavy enough to clear the air, but enough to be an annoyance.

"You want an umbrella?" he said.

I shook my head.

"Look, I'm a pretty poor source on Klein. I worked for Atracor for six years, but it was my start in the industry. They got me straight out of college and they were good to me. They drove me hard, but they tolerated a lot. You never heard of anybody getting fired." He paused, scratching the stubble on his chin. "In fact, looking back and knowing what I know now, that place was an oasis. It had a great atmosphere, not like the City at all. At heart, very academic. Everyone was given all the latitude they wanted. And Klein is generous, really generous."

"He pays well?"

André nodded. "I was paid damn well, and yet I have no idea what contribution I made. I never saw the trades, never saw what we were invested in. I just made my recommendations, like an internal stockbroker, tossing them upstairs into the ether. You never got word of what they thought about anything."

"How did they pay you?"

"Everyone gets a percentage of the performance of the fund. There's no back-stabbing, no horse-trading, no last-minute manoeuvring. You can work out for yourself exactly what you're going to get.

In any other fund, remuneration works like an inverted pyramid. The guy at the top creams off the most, the guys at the next level grab their share, and so it drops to the guy at the bottom who gets only a tiny fraction of what the guy at the top is taking. But Atracor wasn't like that. I earned more there, as a junior, than I've earned as a fund manager at my current hedge fund."

"Sounds like it was a good place to be. Why did you leave?"

He nodded, watching the gleaming asphalt. "The multi-million dollar question. Everyone said I was mad to leave. Atracor was a paradise, but I guess like any paradise it was surreal. I never got a sense that what I was doing actually counted for anything. I had no idea whether my work, and I was working damn hard, had any effect whatsoever on the return of the fund. I was still young, and I wanted to know what I was doing made an impact. I needed that corroboration. I guess it's existential. In Atracor, I had no proof of my existence."

André watched as a car approached, belatedly recognising the driver and waving only after it had passed by. We watched as it turned the corner and disappeared.

"I wanted to prove to myself that I could do it. That I could run my own fund. That I wasn't totally dependent on someone I had never met."

"You were there six years, and you never met Klein?"

"I saw him a good few times, but I never spoke to him. I was never there, in that inner sanctum. The closer you get to the inner circle, the nuttier it gets."

"*Nuttier?*"

"It's like everyone's been drinking the Kool-Aid. I don't mean they're crazy, just focused. Focused and committed. All access to Klein is controlled by his right hand man, Di Pasquantonio. Klein is cerebral, but Di Pasquantonio's an attack-dog. Everyone was terrified of him, even though nobody was ever fired and we were paid damn well.

But we were still afraid. Sounds crazy, doesn't it?" André looked back inside as a door slammed somewhere within the house.

He turned back to me. "Sorry I haven't been of more use. If you're looking for Klein, you've come to the wrong town. Nobody knows where exactly he runs things from, because he wants to stay one step ahead of the regulators. I couldn't tell you, and I was there six years. But I can tell you that if you want to speak to Klein you won't find him in London. You'll find him in New York."

8

"So you went to New York," said Valassis.

Carraway nodded.

"Anyone would have told you to start there in the first place."

"Anyone who knows Klein. Which you do, don't you?"

"Maybe," said Valassis, blowing out a plume of cigar smoke.

"In that case, why don't you tell us what *you're* doing here?"

Valassis took the cigar out of his mouth, examining it with a frown. "That has nothing to do with you."

"You asked why I'm here. It's only fair that I ask the same of you."

"My boat is here."

"Why is your boat here?"

Valassis looked across the river, his bald head glistening in the afternoon light. "Because I want it here. That's the point of having a boat. You can go wherever you damn well like."

"Just for fishing?"

Valassis shrugged. "The sun shines, the women are gorgeous."

"And cheap."

Valassis didn't answer, clearly angry at the remark. I thought he was going to ask Carraway to leave, but instead he took another draw on his cigar, releasing a smoke-ring that drifted under the awning. "So you've found out that much. Go get a woman, and stop wasting our time."

"Carraway hasn't finished his story," I said.

Valassis turned and looked at me, as if he had forgotten that I was there. "What makes you think that he has anything worthwhile to say?"

"I don't. But I've got the time to hear him through."

"Really?" Valassis took a draw on his cigar, releasing a trail of smoke into the air between us. "And what are *you* doing in Vietnam?"

"I'm taking a career break."

"Another one on a 'break'. What does yours entail?"

"I'm doing some writing."

"For what?"

"I don't know yet. I guess I'm looking for a story."

"Perhaps Carraway has something for you," said Jongstra. "That is, if our host will let him to continue?"

We watched as Valassis took another draw on his cigar. He held the smoke in his mouth for a few moments before giving a nod and releasing it across the deck in a grey plume.

Carraway finished the spring roll he was eating and wiped his fingers on a napkin. "I got clearance from Thys to go to New York, telling him I had a lead. In truth, I had no idea of how I was going to track Klein down when I got there.

Basel arranged for me to pay a visit to the SEC when I first arrived. For those of you who don't know, the SEC is the Securities and Exchange Commission. They're the main market regulator in the States, and they're renowned around the world for being the biggest and baddest."

"Baddest?" said Jongstra.

"Meanest. You don't mess with the SEC. Basel was of the opinion that if anyone had something on Klein, it would be them. And we're all supposed to be on the same side, so it was assumed that they would cooperate.

Their New York office is just across the road from where the World Trade Centre once stood. I was shown to a meeting room overlooking that great big hole in the ground. I watched cranes slowly moving back and forth as construction crews prepared the site for the replacement buildings. The project had been held up by a dispute with the World Trade Centre's insurers, who were arguing that the terrorist attack was a single incident, and not two. A little question of having to pay out seven billion dollars, or just three and a half.

After a short wait, the door opened and my contact walked in. He had no jacket or tie, and his sleeves were rolled up. His name was Rafael, he was roughly my age. He didn't look pleased to see me.

"Nobody told me what this is about," he said, shaking my hand.

"It's not routine."

He showed a glimmer of interest. "And?"

"It's an enquiry, of sorts."

"Why have you come to us? Why not the Federal Reserve?"

"This doesn't concern banking."

"What does it concern?"

"Something that's more in your line of work. Hedge funds."

Rafael had pulled out a chair, but instead of sitting down he stood leaning on the back of it. "Hedge funds aren't your territory."

"We're concerned with the stability of the system as a whole. Individual regulators are only looking at their little patch of the woods. Collectively, bigger things could be happening that they just don't see."

Rafael frowned. "You're telling me that the US securities industry is a 'little patch of the woods'?"

"In the context of the global financial system, it is."

"So what have you 'big picture' people discovered?"

"We're still looking into it."

"And how long have you been doing that?"

"A while."

He shook his head. "You're saying nothing. Why should I tell *you* anything?"

"Because we're all in this together. And as Atracor's regulator-"

"Ah!" His eyes lit up. "So it's one fund in particular. Why didn't you say so in the first place? Or do you people in Basel not trust the SEC?"

I shook my head. "We want to start with Atracor, simply because they're the biggest. Then we'll roll it out across the sector as a whole. We're not a regulator, so we're not trying to step on your toes. We're simply trying to connect the dots. Do you have anything relevant that you could fill me in on?"

"What would you term 'relevant'?"

"Anything you think we should know."

Rafael gave a cynical smile. "You want us to do your homework for you?"

"I'd just like to know if there's anything that worries you, as Atracor's lead regulator."

He shook his head. "Atracor is controlled from London."

"That's not what I hear. I hear Klein runs it from New York."

"And where did you hear that?"

"From an ex-employee."

"And how long has this person been an ex-employee?"

"Around five years."

"There's your answer. You're out of date."

"How do you know it's not being run from New York?"

"Klein isn't in New York."

"Where is he then?"

Rafael shrugged. "Why don't you ask him?"

"Because Klein's not going to speak to us." I pushed back my chair and stood up. "Look, the reason we're interested is because we're concerned with the power Klein has in the markets. That's something you should be equally concerned by, no matter what the supposed jurisdiction."

Rafael shrugged. "We all know about the problem. Are you going to add something to it that we didn't already know? We have a whole department looking into it."

"Can I speak to someone from there?"

"You're looking at him."

"And?"

He turned away, walking to the window and looking out at the building site across the street. "This isn't just about Klein. Klein is merely a symptom."

"Of what?"

Rafael looked back at me. "Think about it. According to Economics 101, Klein shouldn't exist. But he does. Consider the Efficient Markets Hypothesis, on which all financial theory is based. Klein is making a mockery of it.""

Carraway paused, looking around as us. "Before anyone asks, let me explain the Efficient Market Hypothesis.

It's the notion that the price of a financial asset will always reflect every available bit of information about it. There's a saying that there are no hundred dollar bills lying about in the street because someone else has already picked them up. It means that nobody should be able to consistently outperform the market."

"Nobody but Klein," said Valassis.

Carraway shook his head. "It all depends on your timeframe. Smart investors manage to beat the market all the time. So do lucky investors. The real test is longevity, which reveals whether it's been just a lucky one-off, or whether there has been real skill behind it all. As they say in German, *einmal ist keinmal*. Anyone can get lucky in the short term. It's the long term that determines true ability. Nobody has been able to do it as consistently as Klein, or for as long as Klein."

"Just as I said," Valassis blew out another plume of smoke. "Nobody but Klein."

"That was Rafael's point. The SEC were sitting there fussing about whether people had crossed the Ts and dotted the Is in their regulatory returns, while Klein was running circles around them."

Valassis smiled. "You can't put a curb on intelligence."

"It's not just about intelligence."

"It's all about intelligence. The smartest people are where the money is. They'll always be where the money is."

"Are you one of those people?" said Carraway.

"I'm retired. And my boat should have left by now. If you want to finish your story, you'd better get on with it."

Carraway took a last sip of beer and put the can down. "Rafael's point was that regulators are only dealing with the part of the financial industry that's visible, and it's shrinking by the day as the unseen bit grows ever larger. I've already talked about Dark Pools, right? Unregulated stock exchanges where you can trade without the outside world seeing.

Capital is also moving away from the regulated banks and insurers, to what is known as the Shadow Banking System. It involves a lot of hedge funds and conduits and other structures which have an advantage over the regulated banks, as they don't have to stick to the rules.

Using the Black Hole analogy which I mentioned earlier, both these elements may be invisible, but they that have grown so large that they exert a gravitational pull on everything else.

Rafael summed it up thus: "The shadow banking system will grow much faster than the regulated banks because it has a level of freedom and flexibility that *we* don't allow."

I'd sat back down in my chair but he remained standing, looking down at me. "Do you know where this is leading?"

I shook my head.

"It's leading to collapse."

"What do you mean?"

"The shadow banking system will grow so big, that one day it will be too big to be allowed to fail. A lot of people think that governments won't bail out hedge funds if they fail, because it's just a bunch of rich people's money. But they'll *have* to be rescued, just like the regulated banks, even though they never played ball in the first place. They'll have to be rescued because if they go down, they take the whole deck of cards with them. They know it, and we know it." Rafael gave a wry smile. "But for us, the issue is much more severe. We've got everything to lose. By 'we' I mean John Doe, the taxpayer. The hedge funds have made their money. Who gets the raw end of the deal? John Doe, every time."

"Not necessarily," I said.

Rafael shook his head. "Check your history. It happens *every* time. There have been plenty of bubbles and just as many crashes, but the market always pulls through because the authorities are forever ready to bail it out.

Hedge funds like Atracor know that. They'll go on to pump up the next bubble, knowing that the authorities will ride to the rescue just as they've always done." Rafael smiled as though he'd just told the punch-line to a joke. "So you see, Klein is not to blame. He's seen the flaws in the system, and he's exploiting them."

"You're saying the rules are inadequate?"

"At best, inadequate. At worst, part of the problem. Right now, they're destabilising things even further. If everyone's following the same rules, they're all having to buy or sell the same assets at the same time, magnifying the effect of a bubble or a crash."

"What's the solution?"

Rafael shook his head. "That's what you people are supposed to prescribe. Here at the SEC, we're just the watchdogs. And we're chained to our kennels while it all passes us by."

"But there are changes underway. There's new legislation-"

"Please!" Rafael started laughing. "Politicians love to go on about policing hedge funds. But how are they actually going to do it? How the hell could we ever analyse the billions of trades executed every year? In any case, as long as there's a free market system it'll always find a way around whatever you put in front of it." He raised his hands in a sign of futility. "We tried to protect the banks, so we banned the short-selling of financial stocks. What has that achieved? Nothing. The easiest way to get around it is to short the index, and buy back every stock other than the financials. And presto, you're short financials, and you're doing it legally."

He paused, standing at the window with the sun streaming in behind him. His dark features, set against the sunlight, gave him a heroic look. But that same sunlight showed up every crease in his crumpled shirt.

"It's completely naive to imagine that we'd ever have any real control over the industry. Its lobbying clout is legendary. The politicians in Washington may be spouting populist rhetoric right now, but underneath it all they won't bite the hand that feeds them."

"It's not just Washington," I said.

"Of course," nodded Rafael. "It's everywhere. Every government wants to have the leading global financial centre, because that's where the tax dollars are. As soon as someone proposes a regulatory tightening, the sector shouts and screams and threatens to leave. That's the problem with globalised finance. Business migrates to where the regulatory controls are lightest.

If New York tightens things up, they'll go to London. If London tightens, they'll go to Hong Kong or Dubai. Every country competes to offer less regulation, because they all want the goose that lays the golden egg.

They don't care where those eggs come from, or if they really are gold at all. Everyone just wants them, plain and simple." He paused, looking out the window. "See over there? That's the New York stock exchange. They're no different. They'll bend over backwards for big hedge funds, turning a blind eye to whatever they're doing. And the best thing is, we made that happen. Stock exchanges used to be de facto monopolies, but we've been encouraging new entrants to provide competition. They all need liquidity, it's the lifeblood of exchanges, and who can give it to them? People like Klein." Rafael smiled again. "When you interfere with an ecosystem, you spawn a whole bunch of unintended consequences."

He checked the phone on his belt and listened to a message. Standing at the window with his shirtsleeves rolled up and the New York skyline behind, he looked like he was ready to take on the world. But that skyline was visible because the two great towers that had been blocking the view were reduced to a hole in the ground.

After a few moments Rafael put away his phone. "They teach you in economics 101 that every participant in the economy behaves rationally. We've always worked on the assumption that everyone in the market aims to make money. They don't go out looking to lose a fortune.

But as it turns out, that's what people did. They wrote mortgages for people who could never pay them back, flipping them on to people who never checked what they were buying. As Keynes said, 'there is nothing so disastrous as a rational policy in an irrational world'."

Rafael walked across to the door. He opened it, turning back to look at me. "We used to have coffee and cookies in the meeting rooms, but they've been taken away. The SEC has a budget, and it's been cut. Our coffee and cookies have been taken away, while those guys are drinking champagne.

By now you will see that there wasn't any point you coming here at all. If Klein is what you're interested in, go and see him. Don't come see us." With that, Rafael walked out of the room, leaving my card on the table.

I picked it up and took an elevator to the ground floor. I stood outside the SEC's offices, watching the cranes in the World Trade Centre site across the road. In four weeks, I had got nowhere.

At that moment, I made a snap decision. The only thing to do was knock on Klein's door. I had no plan, I didn't even know who I would say that I was. The BIS certainly wouldn't have wanted me to barge in there, but I didn't care.

I was sick of it. Sick of everything. Rafael had been right. What exactly were we trying to stand in the way of? In all the weeks that I had been looking, I hadn't come up with anything tangible. I could carry on with it for as long as I liked, and still not come up with anything.

So what were my options? Go back to that office in Basel, and sit there for the rest of my life? In those weeks that I had been out in pursuit of Klein, I'd finally breathed the fresh air that I had originally left London for. Not the change of scenery that I had found in Switzerland. It was about taking charge, and not waiting around for things to happen to me.

So I took a cab from the SEC to Atracor's offices on the Upper East Side. We started along the Hudson River parkway, and were immediately stuck in a traffic jam. I sat there as the cab inched uptown, watching that steely mass of water on my left. You could be forgiven for thinking that the Hudson is a major river, emerging from the heart of a continent. But, like the Thames at Canary Wharf, all you're seeing is an estuary.

It was St Patrick's day, and the annual parade was marching along Fifth Avenue. The traffic got steadily worse, so I eventually got out the cab and walked across town, crossing the procession just south of Central Park.

It was a grey day, similar to that February morning in Basel. But this parade had none of the colour of the Mardi

Gras carnival. Instead of costumes, it was full of people marching in uniforms. Policemen, firemen, soldiers and drum majorettes. And the unions, in their overalls. There were more bagpipers than I've ever seen in Scotland, pumping out their collective wail. A lot of cold bare knees showing beneath those kilts.

Atracor's New York office is housed in a sleek glass building just a block from the East River. As I waited for a receptionist in the lobby, I noted that Atracor occupied three floors. That was a whole lot more office space than they had in the townhouse in St James.

I told the receptionist that I was there to see Klein. She asked for my name and called up to Atracor, relaying my message. After a pause she put the phone down.

"Hold still," she said, pointing the webcam on top of her PC at me.

She took the photo and typed into her keyboard while a printer whirred alongside. She handed me an entry pass, with my blurred face printed on it.

I took the elevator to the eighteenth floor as instructed, having no idea what I was going to say when I got there.

The elevator opened onto an empty reception area, with closed doors at either end. The doors were brightly polished, reflecting multiple images of me that disappeared into infinity. The carpet was springy and I couldn't stand still, slowly moving from one foot to the other. After a few moments the far door clicked open. A man appeared, with close-cropped hair and a pinstripe suit. "Yes?" he said.

I didn't have time to think. What did I have to lose? If Atracor were as secretive as they were purported to be, they wouldn't exactly shout around town that I had come knocking at their door.

"I'm from the Bank for International Settlements, and I'm here to see Dr Klein."

He didn't flinch. "We weren't expecting you," he said.

"I know, but it's important that I speak to Dr Klein. Is he available?"

The man shook his head.

"He's not here?"

"Didn't anyone tell you?"

"Tell me what?"

"Dr Klein doesn't see visitors."

I nodded. "But this is important. If you'll let him know that I'm here, perhaps he'll-"

"Just a moment." The man disappeared back inside, closing the door behind him. I was left standing between the two banks of elevators, listening to the soft pinging as they moved between floors.

After a few minutes the man reappeared, holding a mobile phone against his ear. "You're alone?" he said.

I nodded.

"What about in the lobby? Are there more of you in the lobby?"

"No, just me. I've come all the way from Switzerland."

He stepped back inside, this time leaving the door slightly ajar. I listened while he spoke in a low tone into the mobile and then he reappeared again, slipping it back into his pocket. "Maybe in a couple of days," he said.

"You want me to call?"

The man shook his head. "Dr Klein doesn't take calls."

"I mean the office. Do you have a number I can call?"

The man reached into his jacket pocket. I was expecting a card, but he took out a pen and a scrap of paper, and scribbled something down on it.

He held it out and I walked up and took it from him. There was a number, nothing else.

"Is this yours?" I said.

He nodded.

"What's your name?"

"Just call the number."

"I'm Carraway. Chris Carraway. I'll call in a couple of days."

The man didn't reply as he stepped back through the door, closing it behind him. I stood in the lobby for a few moments, and then took an elevator out of there."

9

"You got to see him?" said Valassis.

"As I just said, I got to leave a message."

"Why the hell are we sitting around, listening to this?" Valassis reached for a beer can, using it to stub out his cigar. "You never got to see him. That's why you're here. You wasted a hell of a lot of time in a wild goose chase after the world's finest investor, and now you're licking your wounds. How old are you, Carraway?"

"Thirty-four."

"Thirty-four, and you've washed up here. The difference between you and us is that we're here by choice. You on the other hand, have no choice at all."

Carraway didn't reply, screwing up his eyes as he looked out across the river. The afternoon sun was just above the opposite bank, sparkling on the water and silhouetting the sampans as they slipped past.

After a few moments he turned back to us. "Let me ask all of you a question. Have things ended up how you expected?"

None of us answered, so he turned to Valassis. "How about you?"

"Of course." Valassis pushed the beer can away.

"And you?" Carraway looked at Jongstra.

"Not exactly. But I've already told you that."

Carraway turned to me. "How about you?"

I shrugged.

"Well, not for me," said Carraway. "Far from it. I always wanted to be a film director. But I studied law at college, because everyone said it was safer.

I came out of there hating law, and decided to follow my dream. I worked hard at a couple of films, but at the end of the day you've got to wait for that lucky break, and in the meantime you need an income. So I started temping at a bank in the City, and it paid surprisingly well. And I waited, and I had an okay life, waiting. The Monday to Friday grind wasn't that bad, even as a temp at the bottom of the food chain.

Working for that bank opened my eyes to a whole world of money that I never knew existed. I was more than happy with what they were paying me, it was so much more than I'd got anywhere else. Until I realised that it was just chicken-feed to them.

And with that realisation, I saw a way up through the cracks of what had looked like a huge incomprehensible machine when I first started. I got to know people, and I knew what to do to crawl my way up. I pulled a few levers, and one day they offered me a permanent position. And not a bad one at that."

Carraway paused, looking at the hawkers on the quayside as they sat watching us. "Deep down I didn't want to take it, because as long as I continued as a temp I was being true to my dream, or true-ish. An artist who doesn't want to starve. So I stalled for a couple of weeks, and during that time I got a huge break. The best lead that I had in the film industry finally came through for me. The one person who I hoped would discover me, called. He had seen my work. This was it.

It was more nervous than a kid on the first day of school as I waited outside his office. Then he called me in, and we chatted for a bit. But I soon realised that he was just being a nice guy. He was trying to cushion the blow. He smiled sympathetically and then he said the hard bit. He tried to do it in a nice way, and I should thank him for that, but he told me that I'd find life a whole lot easier as a mediocre banker than as a mediocre film director.

I thanked him and left, and the next day I accepted the job at the bank. I became permanent, and even though I was doing much better work, getting better paid and moving up the food chain, from that moment I hated it.

And that guy was wrong. To be mediocre in an investment bank is hell. You can survive, in fact you can do quite well if you know how to play the game. But it doesn't stop it being hell. The realisation came five years into the job. What could I do now, a pretence of a banker and a non-existent film director?" Carraway reached for the beer can in front of him, but it was empty and he put it back down.

"Then an opportunity came up with the BIS in Basel. A nice, quiet life." Carraway smiled, shaking his head. "The things you'll do in your thirties that you'd never dream of in your twenties."

"Don't be too hard on yourself," said Jongstra. There are opportunities here. Take my venture, for example. If things get going, we could use you."

"That's very kind," said Carraway. "But you shouldn't offer me anything until you've heard the rest of my story. Mind if I continue?"

Jongstra and I nodded. Valassis leaned back, arms folded.

"As much as I wanted to call, I ended up waiting a week before I phoned the guy at Atracor. I didn't want to lose my chance, but something told me it was better to wait. I felt calm, as if I was in the eye of the financial storm whirling around me. Things were getting worse by the day. There were continued falls in every major stockmarket around the world, and I watched the carnage unfold like it was in slow-motion.

The correlation between markets had everyone especially worried. There's a fundamental principal in finance that you can spread your risk by diversifying across different asset classes. But everything was going down together; stocks, bonds, emerging markets and developed markets. All down the toilet.

And it was no longer just a question of people losing money in the stockmarkets. Just about every major economy was starting to tank too.

Politicians were scrabbling for someone to blame and seized on hedge funds and their manifest greed. They called them locusts, which were driving the world into another great depression and profiting handsomely from it while everyone else crashed and burned.

Greed was to blame, but not just the actions of a greedy few. Everyone had been riding the good times, gorging themselves on cheap debt. Not just those evil hedge funds, but anyone with a mortgage or a credit card or a car loan. And not only consumers, but governments too.

Why would anybody refuse a free lunch? All that debt pushed house prices higher, which meant wealthier consumers who spent more, which meant higher tax revenues, which meant that everyone was winning. The banks, the public, the government.

Now that it had all come crashing down, the most popular line in the media was that someone must have been asleep at the wheel. But that wasn't the case. Anyone who had opened their eyes could have seen what was happening, but nobody wanted the responsibility of taking away the punch bowl while the party was in full swing."

Carraway smiled, watching the hawkers as they finally gave up on us and walked away. "Financial markets have a strange effect on people. Think of any other market, say televisions. If the cost of TV's goes down, people tend to buy more. If the cost goes up, they tend to buy less. It's known as the demand curve, and it reflects the simple logic that the higher the price, the less the demand.

But it's quite the opposite with financial markets. The more the price goes up, the more people want to buy. The higher the greed; the fear of losing out. The lower the price, the less they want to buy. The more the fear of losing everything.

As a result, you'll always get financial bubbles, giving people the opportunity to lose a fortune. They end up deeply ashamed of their cupidity and they lash out, looking for someone to blame. That wonderful presumption peddled very profitably by millions of lawyers that for every misfortune, someone must be to blame. The public never blames itself.

In spite of the gathering outcry, none of the hedge funds were answering their critics. None of them are known by the general public anyway. There was no Bastille that could be stormed, because they're scattered around the world in anonymous offices. And in their minds, they were still the Masters of the Universe, answerable to no one.

But I was going to see the best of them. I told Thys that I had a direct lead to Klein, without telling him how I obtained it. He wasn't happy. He told me that my remit was not to approach Klein directly, but simply to find out more about him. That was contrary to his original instructions. I guess Thys wanted the honour of meeting Klein for himself. He said that if I got a meeting, I was to call him immediately. In the meantime, he wanted me to see the other big hedge funds while I was in New York.

Most of the funds agreed to see me at short notice, but from the start of the very first meeting it was clear that I was dealing with spokespeople, not real decision makers.

The guy I met in my first meeting was right at the bottom of his hedge fund, but as far as he was concerned he sat at the same table as the Masters of the Universe and his distain for me showed. After all, who was I? Just some petty official, hopelessly outclassed and at best irrelevant.

I was already sick of my second-class status by the next meeting, which, like the first, was going nowhere. They had fielded a PR person to meet me. Whoever heard of a PR person in a hedge fund? But he thought he was something special. A hedge fund nobody, and yet he thought he was great.

He gave me no real answers. He didn't even try to make it look like he cared, or that he wanted to help. The meeting was a sham and I was the fool for sitting there, listening to his crap.

I was about to stand up and walk out, but instead I did something else. I let slip that I was seeing Klein next. I have no idea why I said it, maybe I just wanted a way to exit the meeting without looking like a complete sap. The PR man snapped to attention.

"Atracor?" he said. "You're seeing Atracor?"

"Klein," I said. "I'm seeing Klein. I have a regular meeting with him."

"What's his take on this?" The man's smugness had disappeared.

I frowned. "*This*?" It was my turn to be obtuse.

"This. This situation."

"I really can't say. You wouldn't want me telling him anything *we've* discussed, would you?"

"No. No, of course not."

"We value partners like that," I said, standing up.

"Partners?" he said.

"That's right."

He rushed after me as I walked to the door. "Obviously we want to be of as much help as we can," he said.

"Obviously," I said, leaving the room.

He followed after me as I headed down the corridor. "The elevators are that way," he said.

"I'm not going to the elevators. I'm going to the bathroom."

"Sure, it's right there. On your left."

"I went inside and stayed for some time, smiling at myself in the mirror. When I came out, he was still standing there. I walked straight past him to the elevators.

"Everyone's really busy around here," he said as he followed behind. "You know, the way the markets are. But we value keeping a good relationship with people like the-" he checked my card, "the BIS. I'm sure one of our investment managers could see you, later in the week. Or our CIO. Maybe even our CIO, but I'll have to check."

"Who is your CIO?" I said, stopping alongside the elevators. CIO means Chief Investment Officer. Amazing how hedge funds are starting to sound like corporations.

He told me a name. I made it clear that it meant nothing to me.

I left their offices, ignoring the man's outstretched hand. He said he would come back with some times for a meeting. I was non-committal, even bored.

Those meetings were pointless, but I had found a way to enjoy them. And I was really starting to enjoy them. In each of the meetings that followed, I allowed myself to be subject to the usual condescension from whoever they had placed in front of me. And then I mentioned Klein.

I loved the alacrity with which things then changed. I started letting my little secret drop earlier, instead of saving it for the end. Not because I intended to get more useful information as a result, not at all. It was all pointless. But it would feed my ego. And my ego, having never been fed, loved it and wanted more.

Towards the end of that week of meetings, another bank went under. Fuldman, Bensinger & Lay was much larger than Schwartz Greenberg, but this time the authorities did nothing to save it. Either they had decided to teach the market a lesson, or they couldn't find anyone big and brave enough to take it over. Whichever, it was a huge mistake. It sent a heart attack through the financial system.

It started in the least expected, most innocuous corner of the markets. No one had any reason to imagine that something bad might happen there. Sure, bad things might happen in Argentine debt, or in junk bonds, or Russian banks or a gold mine in Papua New Guinea where the chief geologist has just been thrown out of the company helicopter. There, maybe. But not the money markets. And that's where the liquidity crisis started. Right there under our noses in the small, overlooked, day-to-day stuff.

The money market is also known as the commercial paper market. It's regarded as the equivalent to cash. It's as good as cash, as safe as cash. When you make a deposit into a money market fund, as far as you're concerned it's the equivalent of a bank deposit. A bank deposit earning a slightly higher interest rate, because there's a *slightly* higher risk involved. But no one ever concerned themselves about that. Until the day the entire market seized up.

After Schwartz Greenberg was rescued, all the major money market funds loaded up on commercial paper issued by investment banks, taking the view that it was effectively underwritten by the government. Whatever the risk, these banks wouldn't be allowed to fail. It sent the wrong message.

Those funds that were holding Fuldman paper 'broke the buck', as they call it. If you put one hundred dollars into a money market fund, you expect to get one hundred dollars back, plus interest. But the Fuldman paper that these funds were holding was now worthless, and to make matters worse, just how many other Fuldmans were in there, about to blow up as well?

There was a stampede as people tried to pull out of money market funds, but they couldn't. Just like a bank, these funds aren't run on the assumption that they have to pay back every single deposit tomorrow. They are invested in commercial paper with maturities of anything between thirty to ninety days, and they quite simply have to wait for funds to mature. In the meantime you have people hammering on the door, going nuts.

So the commercial paper market seized up. We're talking about a huge market, which every major company uses to manage daily liquidity. When it came to a shuddering halt, perfectly healthy companies lost control of their day-to-day cashflow. That meant not paying salaries, or their suppliers.

Almost overnight, strange things started to happen. International trade came to a virtual standstill, as no bank would issue a letter of credit to a customer who they thought couldn't repay them. And the customer's suppliers weren't going to put anything on a ship and send it across the ocean if they didn't get that letter of credit first.

Within weeks a big proportion of the world's cargo fleet was standing idle. And car sales plunged. Nobody's going to go out and buy a car if they don't know whether they'll have a job at the end of the month, or, even if they have a job, whether they'll get paid. And all those suppliers who make the things that go into a car were hit, and their suppliers too.

Right in the middle of all this, I received a call. It was a hedge fund from the list I had been given, who hadn't previously bothered to get back to me. Returning the compliment, I pretended not to remember. They were persistent, suggesting a meeting with a senior partner.

It was a large and prestigious fund, just a few blocks from Atracor. In fact, you could see Klein's offices from the meeting room that I was shown to. I didn't have to wait long before the door opened behind me and a Master of the Universe entered, complete with bald head, grey goatee and red braces.

He barely looked at me. Even though they had requested the meeting, he let me do the talking. I gave him the usual spiel, but I made it extra sugary. I explained that we were looking for more openness, a greater understanding between ourselves and the hedge fund community.

I love it when they use the term 'community' for something that is anything but. To succeed in that world you have to tread on everyone else, while they're trying to do the exact same thing to you.

This very important man sitting in front of me was someone who wouldn't usually have the time or the patience to listen to all that crap. But I made him sit through it, because for once I had the power."

"What do you mean?" said Jongstra.

Carraway smiled. "I'd finally worked out why people do this."

"Do what?"

"I'm someone who wanted to be an artist but didn't want to starve, so I ended up in a world where I didn't belong, and which I've never understood. I went along with it, just like most people go along with their lot in life, but I never understood it at all. I was really just coasting along, looking for the easiest deal, where I could get through a five day week as painlessly as possible." Carraway picked up his beer can, shook it and put it back down. "Is there any more beer?"

Valassis didn't answer. He hadn't shown much interest in Carraway before, but he was watching him closely now.

"I take it that's a no. I guess you've got to be going soon." Carraway smiled. "Where was I? Oh yes, surrounded by people quite unlike myself. Ambitious, hardworking, determined. I'd never really understood what makes them want to get out there and work their nuts off and take on all that stress. There's the money, of course. But it can't be just that. There has to be more to it.

I mean, above a certain amount, money doesn't really mean a hell of a lot. So why do they do it? Why do they keep pushing that extra yard, beyond which they're already comfortable and safe and secure?"

He looked around at us, but no one answered.

"The answer is power. They do it for the power. It was only when I tasted it, that I finally understood. Now I had it. People were paying attention to me, looking at me in a completely new light. I was someone. Right from the beginning I had been content to slip though life a nobody, doing the right thing, keeping my head down. But now, suddenly I was someone. I had used a bit of guile, and I was *someone*. And my guile was being steadily transformed from a white lie to a misrepresentation to a potential fraud, and it felt great. I was simply doing what all those other people did." Carraway looked at Jongstra. "Does that answer your question?"

He nodded. "I guess it does."

"On with the story then. I blathered for some time, until the very important man from the very important hedge fund cut me short.

"I believe you've seen Klein," he said.

I didn't reply.

"Well?"

"It's not something we comment on."

"How's he doing?"

"I smiled at such a ridiculous question. I looked at the man's card on the table in front of me, as if I'd already forgotten his name. "How about you?"

His eyes narrowed. "I asked you a question. How's he doing?"

"Oh, he's fine. And you?"

The man took a long pause, before replying "We're okay."

So they weren't okay. They weren't okay at all. "Good to hear," I said, as condescendingly as possible.

"What do you want?" said the man. He had appeared so controlled and measured at first, but he was clearly stressed. I was consuming time that he didn't have.

"I'm trying to get a feel for where you're at, what you're seeing. How you're doing."

"I just said we're doing fine."

"And what are you seeing?"

"The same as anyone else." Ordinarily someone like this would have thrown me out by now. But this man was desperate. Otherwise he quite simply wouldn't have been sitting there with me.

"Tough markets," I said. "Very tough. They'll take some people down."

"What's it to you?"

"We're concerned about systemic risk to the system. If a big hedge fund were to go under, it could drag others down like a-"

"So what are you doing about it?"

I gave him the smile of a bureaucrat who can be relied upon to do nothing other than waste your time. "That's why I'm here. We're looking into it."

"Jesus! What part this do you not understand? Have you got fuck-all else to do?" He picked up his Blackberry as it pinged on the table in front of him. He frowned as he read the message. "Well?" he looked up at me.

I gave a casual shrug. "We can see what goes on with the major banks, but not much beyond that. Hence the term, the 'shadow banking system', which hedge funds are a big part of."

He shook his head. "It's those banks of yours that are the problem. Everything would be fine, if it wasn't for those idiots."

I watched him for a few moments before replying, smiling inwardly. Yes indeed, they weren't fine at all. "Those banks may be idiots, but you were happy for them to shovel cheap credit at you. Until you discover that idiocy works both ways."

He looked up, pointing his Blackberry at me. "Who the fuck do you think you are? What the fuck have you people done, other than compound the problem? Your capital requirements are screwing everything up."

"Let me stop there for a moment," said Carraway, looking around at us. "Just so that everyone here knows, the Bank for International Settlements sets capital ratios that just about every bank in the world must comply with. If a bank is in danger of breaching those ratios, it will have to either raise capital or reduce its assets. Raising capital would not be a bank's first choice, so they'll almost always reduce assets.

As banks were taking hits from the market, they were trying to shore up their BIS ratios by raising collateral requirements and pulling in credit lines. They did this especially with hedge funds, as the BIS ratios are risk-weighted and therefore penalise higher risk assets.

Highly leveraged hedge funds had to respond by selling assets. This in turn added to the selling pressure, causing prices to fall more, which further reduced the level of collateral, causing banks to demand more, which caused more selling, leading to a vicious circle. A 'death spiral' is what some people called it."

"How did they pull out of it?" I asked.

"Just as the SEC guy said. In effect, Joe Public rode to the rescue. His tax dollars were pressed into action, preventing a meltdown." Carraway smiled. "The Masters of the Universe were saved by the common man."

"Although he had no say in it."

Carraway nodded. "Isn't that always the case?"

"Which leaves the Masters of the Universe back in charge. The one sitting opposite me was unrepentant. I explained to him that the very reason for the BIS's capital requirements was to stop banks from going under. I couldn't believe that I was actually defending the BIS. But against that sort of person it was understandable.

He shook his head. "You're nailing life preservers onto drowning men. Doesn't do anyone any good."

I frowned in mock concern. "Just for clarity, are you saying that our capital requirements are causing you problems?"

"They are causing the market problems."

"So not you specifically, then."

He didn't answer, picking up the Blackberry as it pinged again. I watched as he scrolled through the messages.

"You still haven't told me about Klein," he said without looking up.

"I said he's fine."

He looked at me. "Don't give me that crap. People like Klein are in deep shit. All those black-box trading models are in trouble right now, because they've ended up doing the exact same thing. If you feed data into computers in search of anomalies, they're going to come back with the exact same answers."

He looked at me as if to seek confirmation, which told me that he had no idea if Klein really was in trouble. But he hoped that he was.

I didn't say anything. He looked down again, rolling the wheel on the Blackberry with his thumb even though no new messages had come in.

"So?" I said after a few moments, trying not to smile. "Do you have a problem?"

I could see that he wanted to tell me more, but he needed to know that he had my confidence. Here was a Master of the Universe, needing something from me. Inwardly, I was beaming. I would make him beg. But I'd give him an opener first. "Everything that we discuss in this room is confidential. You should know that."

He picked up my card and looked at it again. He had made this meeting confrontational, and now he needed to steer it in another direction. Did I help him? Of course I didn't. I pushed back my chair as if I was about to go.

He looked up. "If a major hedge fund goes down, it'll take your precious banks with it. No matter what arbitrary capital requirements you've slapped on them. It won't save them."

"You may well be right," I said, looking as if I really didn't care. What I had learned from my time in investment banking is that you should always be prepared to walk away from a deal. That puts you in the best possible negotiating position.

"Well?" he said. "What are you going to do about it?"

I raised an eyebrow. "You're saying that you people need our help?"

"I'm saying that the whole financial system is fucked unless somebody does something. And if the financial system is fucked, then everything is fucked. It takes the global economy down with it."

"So you care about the world," I said.

He glared at me, tossing my card onto the table. "Who the fuck do you think you are? What exactly do you want?"

"As I said, we're trying to find out where the damage is."

"Are you fucking blind? It's everywhere."

I shook my head. "Not everywhere. It's-"

"You don't have a fucking clue. And you're wasting my time."

I was losing the conversation. I was no match for him, I never would be. But I'd learned to lie. I took a punt. "We believe you're in trouble," I said, leaning back in the chair.

"Who's been saying that?"

I shrugged.

"Has Klein been telling you that?"

"More like a hunch."

"You came to the wrong place. Find some other fund to put the shackles on."

"Very well." I stood up.

He looked up at me. "Klein is more leveraged than the rest of us. Everyone knows that."

"Klein is not a problem."

He stared at me. "Have you bailed him out?"

"I couldn't possibly say."

"There's no way he can still be afloat, with all that debt he has to roll over. What deal did you do with him?"

"The BIS only deals with banks."

"The fuck it does. Klein's exposure is bigger than any bank. How much have you given him?"

I shook my head. "Like I said, it isn't Klein who we're worried about."

"Then who?"

"Why do you think I'm here?"

His eyes sharpened with a glint of opportunity. It's always opportunity with these people. I was going to enjoy making him work for something that wasn't there. "If you tell me the problem, maybe I can help."

He watched me for a few moments, his jaw set. "I don't want this getting out. I sure as fuck don't want this getting out. Do you hear me?"

"You have my total confidence. That's why I'm here. We're trying to prevent contagion. It is not in our interests, or anyone's interests, for it to get out."

He sat watching me for a few moments, suddenly looking very tired.

"What do you need?" I was surprised by how soothing my voice could be.

He looked down. "Are you prepared to extend credit lines, if a hedge fund requests it?"

"It depends whether or not we have a relationship," I replied. In truth, I had no idea. It was nothing to do with me. But I could smell fear, and I loved it.

He looked up at me. "You have a relationship with Klein?"

I didn't answer. By not answering, I meant yes.

"How much have you given him?"

"As I said, Klein is absolutely fine. But tell me, won't your banks extend you credit?"

He didn't answer at first, looking around the room. "It's happening to everyone," he said after a few moments. "We're all having to sell."

I nodded in commiseration. "How much do you need?"

He shifted in his chair, looking quite uncomfortable. For once, he didn't have a ready answer. I smiled again. He needed so much from me.

"Give me a call when you've worked it out," I said, and walked out the room."

"How much did he need?" said Valassis.

Carraway shrugged. "I told him to call me."

"And?"

"He did, several times."

"So how much did he need?"

"I have no idea. I never returned his calls."

10

We looked up as the boat juddered against its fenders.

"Lan!" called Valassis.

We waited in silence until she appeared in the doorway.

"Where are they?"

"They come now."

"You said that fifteen minutes ago. "Where the hell are they?"

"They come now-now."

"If they're not here in five minutes there's going to be shit, you hear me?"

She didn't reply, disappearing back into the cabin.

This time Valassis didn't need to stand as he scanned the crowd on the quayside. The yacht's deck was almost level with the quay.

"That's one hell of a tide," said Jongstra. "Look how far it's come in already."

Valassis nodded. "There's a four metre tidal difference in the delta. An incoming tide can invert the Mekong's flow all the way to Phnom Penh."

"But that's four hundred kilometres away."

"As you said, it's one hell of a tide." Valassis turned to Carraway. "And it is one that I will be sailing on. So I suggest you finish your story."

He had just taken a bite from the last spring roll, and sat chewing for a few moments before swallowing. "When I called Atracor a week later, the person who answered wasn't the guy I had spoken to before. He didn't seem to know anything about it. I explained who I was, and asked if Klein was ready to see me.

Without saying anything, he put me on hold. I was expecting to be cut off, but then he was back on the line. He told me to go to Connecticut.

"Dr Klein is in Connecticut?" I said.

"He will see you there."

I asked for the address and was put on hold again. He came back with an address in Greenwich, Connecticut. I asked him when Klein wanted to meet me.

"Go there now," he said.

I walked the few blocks between my hotel and Grand Central station. On the way I passed Fuldman's head office, its doors locked. The bank was now in the hands of administrators which were handling its bankruptcy.

I forgot to mention that Glenn worked for Fuldman. I remember him telling me just how much Fuldman had paid to poach him from his previous employer. By then he had accumulated a huge amount of stock options, reflecting a very successful career, so Fuldman had to make good those and more. And how did they do it? By giving him even more stock options. Stock options in Fuldman, Bensinger & Lay. Stock options that were now worthless. When the news of Fuldman broke, I had thought of giving Glenn a call, but I didn't need him any more. And it's never good to gloat.

I took a train from Grand Central to Greenwich. I read in the Wall Street Journal that the world's central banks had wheeled out their big guns in response to the crisis. They were buying commercial paper that everyone else was dumping, effectively printing money to pay for it. There were rumours that the Fed would print over a trillion dollars to bail out the banks, and maybe some car companies too.

The train journey took just under an hour. We passed through an endless suburban sprawl until we arrived at Greenwich, which is at the southernmost tip of Connecticut and has a country feel to it.

The fact that Greenwich is greener and more pleasant than New York may go some way to explaining why so many hedge funds are located there, but the real reason is tax. Like all big cities, New York routinely runs into debt and would dearly love to tax deep-pocketed hedge funds, if they were there.

I took a taxi from the station to the address I had been given. It was a big house, set some way back from the road. The trees out front were blackened and bare, as if they were made of the same iron as the fence barring the property from the outside world.

I got out of the cab and pressed the buzzer on the gate. The sun was shining and the lawn out front was a dazzling green. But the house itself was dark. Black granite, with slate roofing. The windows gleamed in the sunlight, but revealed nothing of what was inside.

Finally a voice answered on the intercom. I said who I was. After a pause the gates swung slowly inwards, scraping a leaf across the asphalt. I started up the driveway, noticing several pieces of paper attached to the fence posts which were fluttering in the breeze,

I felt like a door-to-door salesman as I approached the house. For some reason, I had brought my briefcase. I hardly ever take it with me, but I had brought it this time, as if I needed something to hold. As I walked up the drive, the waters of Long Island Sound emerged behind the house, sparkling in the sunlight. The property ran down to the water's edge, where there was a jetty and a boathouse.

I stopped outside the front door and rang the bell. The man who answered looked at me for a few moments and then smiled. "Come in," he said, as if I were a neighbour stopping by for a chat.

I followed him past a huge spiral staircase into a reception room that probably hadn't been updated since the eighties. The upholstery was cream, and the deep-pile carpet a faded green. The room smelt musty, with all the windows closed. The blinds on one side had been lowered, but not the others. The low-angled sun shone right in, unchecked.

The man sat down on a sofa that was out of the sun, and I took the chair opposite. He was about my age, with black-rimmed glasses and a goatee.

"We don't get visitors very often," he said.

I nodded. "I appreciate Dr Klein agreeing to see me. I haven't been able to explain exactly-"

"Yes, yes," he waved his hand. "We know all about that."

We sat in silence for a few moments, while a clock ticked above the fireplace. I thought I could hear the shouts of children in the distance, as if there was a playground outside.

"Sorry," I said, "I didn't catch your name."

He smiled. "Vance."

"Vance-?"

"Just Vance. We're all on first name terms here."

"You work with Dr Klein?"

He looked up at the ceiling for a few moments, fluttering his eyelids as he looked back down. "If only," he said.

I turned around as footsteps pattered across the marble floor out in the entrance hall. A little boy ran into the room. He stopped and looked at us, and then ran out again, shouting something. He was dressed like any American kid, but he looked Somalian or Ethiopian.

"You're a relative of Dr Klein?" I said, turning back to Vance.

He looked down, smiling demurely. "I'd like to think so."

"I appreciate that Dr Klein has agreed to see me at his home. I was prepared to meet at the office."

"This is the office."

"But what about Atracor's offices in London and New York?"

"They're part of it. But this, this is the epicentre. This is where it all happens. " He looked around the room, as if he were seeing it for the first time. "After all, that's why you're here. No?"

I nodded. "You could say that."

We sat in silence, accompanied by the ticking clock, and I wondered just how many billions were being lost in world markets while we waited in that quiet cocoon.

"What do you do here?" I said after a few moments.

Vance didn't reply, looking straight ahead as if he hadn't heard me speak.

"Is there anything you'd like to know about me?"

He shook his head.

"Wouldn't you like to know why I'm here?"

He smiled again. "We know why you're here."

"Who told you?"

"Give Dr Klein some credit. Why wouldn't he know?" Vance stood up and walked across to the window. He remained to one side, out of the sun. "After all, you wouldn't come calling here if you didn't have a notion of the kind of man he is. Of course he knows why you are here."

"Well, I appreciate him seeing me."

Vance looked back, shaking his finger at me. "Not so fast. He'll decide when it's time."

I turned around as a door slammed somewhere down the passage, followed by children's laughter. I looked back at Vance but he was gazing out of the window with screwed-up eyes, silhouetted by the sparkling water of Long Island Sound.

"Is there anything you'd like to know in the meantime?" I said.

He shook his head. "It's all about what *you* need to know. After all, that's why you're here. Not the other way round."

"Maybe it's better if I explain exactly-"

He held up his hand. "Remember one thing. You don't talk to Dr Klein. You listen."

As he spoke, the door at the far end of the room creaked open and two little girls looked out from behind it, giggling softly. One was Latina, the other Asian.

"Do you have any idea of the sort of man Dr Klein is?" said Vance, ignoring them.

"That's what I'm here to find out."

Vance nodded approvingly, walking back to the sofa. He sat back down, adopting a different posture to the one he had before. This time he sat upright while his pale thin fingers drummed lightly on his thighs. "Let me give you a little primer. Dr Klein is the sort of man who comes only once a generation. That's just about all humanity can produce. For the rest of the time, it contents itself with pumping out mediocrity." Vance smiled again. "Do you know what that means?"

I shook my head.

"It means you have to side with the genius. The genius will always win."

We both looked up as the far door swung open, banging against a chair. A bunch of children ran across the room, maybe ten in all. A mixture of black, white, Asian and Latino. They burst into giggles as they ran past us, stirring up dust that hung in the air, so that the sunlight streaming through the windows was transformed into blocks of light.

Vance sat watching the door to the entrance hall for some time after they had disappeared, as if ensuring they were gone. "Dr Klein is first and foremost a scientist. He's not a money-man, he's not just another wall-street baron. He is a man of science."

"But isn't it ultimately about the money?"

Vance frowned at me. "What do you mean?"

"Why Dr Klein does this, why all of you do this. It's the money."

Vance shook his head. "Not at all. If money is your primary motivation, you will fail. Money is about greed, and greed is an emotion." He smiled again. "Tell me. On your journey to see us, no doubt you paid a visit to Leon Rom?"

I nodded.

"Then you'll know that Mr Rom is almost as good as Dr Klein. But not good enough. Otherwise you would have been content to see him, and look no further. Tell me, why is he not good enough?"

I shrugged.

"Leon Rom is highly intelligent, extremely driven, and very successful. But he can't help being human. The media have decried hedge fund managers like him as monsters, devoid of humanity. But Leon Rom *is* human. He is an emotional man. Emotion is the enemy of successful trading."

Vance seemed to relax a little, sitting back in the sofa and crossing one leg over the other. "Atracor began as a research lab that happened to make investments. It was all about building the right algorithms, never about the money. Money was simply a by-product." Vance waved his hand dismissively around the room. "People talk about Dr Klein all the time, but none of them speaks the truth. All you ever hear is the money, how he's manipulating the markets, how he's the dreaded figurehead of ultra-capitalism. That couldn't be further from the truth.

He's a philanthropist. He's on the boards of many non-profit organisations, most of which have entrusted him with their endowments." Vance looked up to the ceiling, shaking his head. "But does anyone mention that? No, because that's not what they're interested in. They all say they hate money, but would any of them give it away as readily as Dr Klein has? No way. They're obsessed with money. Even the people who say they aren't. Even the supposed socialists and tree-huggers and the anti-globalisation crowd. Always money, money, money." Vance paused for a moment. "But you're not. Or are you?"

I shook my head. "I'm just a salaried employee."

"No harm in that. No harm at all. You do an honest day's work. Dr Klein respects that." Vance paused, his face clouding over. "But if you'd come round here just like everyone else, sniffing for money, you would never have been let in." He jabbed the sofa cushion with his finger. "Never."

The two girls had snuck back into the room and were sidling up to us. Vance followed my line of sight as I watched them. "You're wondering about the children."

I nodded.

"They're Dr Klein's kids. He adopts deserving children from all over the developing world. Bright kids who would otherwise have no future."

"They go to school?"

"They don't need school. They've got the most intelligent man in the world giving them his time and attention. They'll all go on to do great things when they go back home."

"Isn't this their home?"

"It is, for now. But eventually we all have to go out into the world. Unlike their brethren emerging from orphanages, these children will go on to do great things." Vance smiled at me. "Dr Klein will see to that."

The two girls stood in silence, watching us a few feet from the sofa.

"That's how you sort out the world's problems. You invest in talented kids, and when they get older, put them in a position to make changes. That's the mind of an investor. Compound your return. These kids will go on to raise a generation after them, and so on." Vance reached out and grabbed the black girl. She screamed with laughter as he pulled her onto his lap. "This is Aurelia, from Burkina Faso." He stroked her hair, and looked up at me. "Do you know where Burkina Faso is?"

I shook my head.

"No reason why you should. There's nothing there, just a chunk of desert scrub carved out of former French West Africa. But the chances are very good there's oil. You'll need a pipeline to get it to the coast, but there's already one going in from Chad next door, so you can tap into that, and presto!" Vance jiggled the girl on his knee and she burst out giggling.

"Aurelia will be a part of that. Before she came here, her only future would have consisted of picking through scraps in a garbage heap. But now she's going to be a part of something so much greater."

Vance sat forward and put her down. She ran out of the room, followed by the other girl.

When they were gone, Vance turned back to me, smoothing his trousers. "What did you expect to find here?"

I shrugged. "I really don't know. To be honest, I was getting nowhere and it was my last-"

"But you've heard so much! Everyone has something to say about Dr Klein. You must have formed an opinion."

"I've heard a hell of a lot, but it hasn't led anywhere. That's why I'm here, because I don't feel I've been able to make any judgement at all about the man himself."

Vance smiled. "You expect to find an ego here. A huge, monstrous ego."

I nodded. "Something like that."

"Hardly surprising. Wall Street is all about egos. Obscene, inflated egos, and Dr Klein has bettered them all. For that, he must have the most grotesque ego of all. Right?"

Vance was on a roll, and to keep him going I gave him the reply he wanted. "Yes," I said. "That would make sense."

"Wrong! Dr Klein isn't interested in money. He's not interested in money, and yet he's beaten every one of them and they are driven by it. So you see?"

"No I don't," I said, shaking my head.

"Ego blinds people. Dr Klein sees the truth."

Vance stood up again and crossed the room, pushing the door closed. As he was about to return to the sofa, the handle started to turn and he whipped around, pulling the door open. "Not now," he said to the little girl standing there. "We're busy."

He closed the door and stood with his hands on his hips. "Do you have any idea just how privileged I am to be here? To bear witness to genius? That man has enlarged my mind."

"You're very lucky indeed," I said, once again giving him the reply he wanted.

"Luck?" Vance smiled as if I was a kindred spirit. "Interesting you should say that. If you analyse it, ninety percent of life is luck. I'm not talking about the everyday stuff that you can get right if you stick with it and stay out of trouble. I'm talking about the big events. A really big windfall, just like a really big disaster, is basically down to chance. And that's where it gets interesting."

"How so?" I said.

Vance returned to the sofa and sat down, crossing his legs again. "The two events have essentially the same cause, but people interpret them very differently. When it's a disaster, people sit around in bewilderment and say 'Why? Why me?' But if it's a windfall, they stand with their chest out and marvel at how smart they are, how they made it happen. Hence, the ego. The ego makes it all explicable. The ego makes you stupid. It blinds you to the truth."

Vance reached over to the coffee table and picked up a copy of the Wall Street Journal. "Look at the headlines. You can smell the fear. Amazing how all that greed dissolved so quickly into panic. They're all blaming Dr Klein, aren't they?"

"Something like that," I said.

"And that's why you're here."

I shook my head. "Not exactly. I never actually cleared it with my boss. You could say it's partly for personal reasons."

Vance liked my reply. He laughed, slapping his thigh with the newspaper. "They're all blaming Dr Klein because they're frightened. What is the greatest fear? Fear of the unknown." He sat watching me. I guess he was expecting a response, so I nodded.

"And what is unknown?"

I shrugged, shaking my head.

"All those so-called Wall Street gurus with their inflated egos have been living by greed alone, while Dr Klein has been patiently modelling end-game scenarios. Those disasters where you lose everything. An event so bad, such that people cannot imagine it happening. So it won't happen, it can't happen. Or more correctly, it's something people simply couldn't stomach happening, so they're forever blind to the possibility.

When the market was at its peak, Dr Klein was the only man preparing for armageddon. Everyone would have said that was crazy, but look where we are now." Vance gave a satisfied smile, tossing the paper onto the coffee table. "The unimaginable has come to pass." He paused, seeming to focus on me for the first time. "I know what you're thinking. What about us? Where is Atracor in all of this?

I nodded.

"Quite simply we're profiting from the very event that is sinking lesser firms." Vance glanced at his watch. "And on that subject, I've got to get back to work." He stood up, dusting the front of his trousers. "You look surprised. What do you think we do, sit around all day? The people behind the most successful hedge fund in the world just sit around, and beat everyone at their own game?"

I shook my head. "I guess not."

"Dr Klein is a workaholic. The man never stops. I've never seen anyone who could keep up with him." Vance looked towards the far door, which was still ajar and gave a view of the staircase. "That's why he's up there, on his own. But before I go, any questions?"

"Not right now," I said. "You've given me a lot to think about."

He nodded. "Well you sit there and think about it."

"There is one thing," I said as he was about to go.

"Yes?"

"Along the fence, out front. When I arrived here, I couldn't help noticing the pieces of paper. What is that?"

"An exercise in futility."

"What do you mean?"

"Those are subpoenas."

"Really?"

He smiled. "Don't think you're the first to try get in here. They've tried to serve Dr Klein with plenty of subpoenas, but they can never find him." Vance glanced out a window that looked onto Long Island Sound. "It could be different if they had some imagination, but they don't. I mean, why would he ever leave here by the front, when there's a dock out back?"

"You trust me enough to tell me that?"

Vance turned back to me and smiled. "You're not going anywhere right now, are you?" He walked across the room, leaving me in my chair.

"Should I just wait here?" I called after him.

Vance stopped at the door. "You might as well."

"Do you know how long Dr Klein will be?"

Vance shrugged, shaking his head. "There's no way of knowing. You can be like everyone in the market, trying to second-guess him, but I wouldn't advise it. You'll never know, just as they'll never know. Quite simply, Dr Klein will see you when he sees you."

Vance was about to pull the door shut behind him, but instead he looked back into the room. "Take the long term view, and know that all good things come to those who wait. That is, if you can avoid the accidents along the way."

With that he was gone, the door clicking softly shut behind him."

11

The awning above us had long ceased to provide any cover from the sun. We were sweating just like those people on the quay, but they earned it. We sat and watched a nation on the move. Scooters and motorbikes and Tuk-Tuks criss-crossing the concrete in front of us, loaded with baskets, trussed chickens and ducks, polystyrene blocks, bundles of fabric, sacks of rice.

"Incredible," said Jongstra. "They never stop."

"What do you expect?" said Valassis. "They have nothing."

"You're wrong," said Carraway. "They get four rice harvests a year. That makes the Mekong delta one of the most productive farmlands in the world."

"Not for much longer," said Valassis.

"Why do you say that?"

"Most of this delta will be submerged in ten years."

Carraway shook his head. "Something will be done about it. People are rallying around climate change. It's fast becoming the world's biggest political issue."

Valassis turned to look at him. "You think a bunch of rice farmers have the power to change anything?"

"It's not just about rice farmers."

"Of course it is. An extra degree in temperature means they're flooded, but that doesn't mean a hell of a lot for anyone else." Valassis turned to the quayside again. "Just look at them. This is why you invest in Asia, because they've got nothing and they're hungry to get ahead. They want something of what we have. They want a TV and an air conditioner and a car, and if that means some rice farmers get flooded, what do they care? Why should anyone care? Because TVs and air conditioners and cars are what moves the economy, not rice."

"Not for much longer," said Carraway.

"You're the one who doesn't have much longer. Get on with it. Did you, or did you not meet Klein?"

Carraway smiled. "Don't worry. This hour hasn't been in vain. I got to see him. But I had to wait for two weeks."

"You sat in the house for two weeks?"

"I waited there all afternoon that first day, and as it was getting dark Vance reappeared and said they would make up a room for me. He showed me to a bedroom with an en-suite bathroom. He even gave me a change of clothes.

I waited the whole of the next day, reading the papers and watching TV, wearing the polo shirt and chinos that Vance had given me. I dozed off on the sofa after lunch and woke to find a line of children staring at me. I tried to engage them, but a Filipino woman came in and shooed them away.

Aside from the kids, there were quite a few adults in the house. They were mostly Latino and kept to themselves. No one would look me in the eye, let alone speak to me, but you got a sense that they all knew Klein had invited me there. There were security guards too. I hadn't seen any when I arrived, but every now and then I noticed them passing by a window, patrolling the grounds. They never came into the house.

It was clear that everyone there worked in the household, and not for Atracor itself. I got a sense that Vance was someone like me, who had arrived there seeking Klein and had ended up never leaving, believing that he was a part of it.

Nobody seemed to be on any particular schedule. There were no fixed mealtimes, with everyone helping themselves in the kitchen. It was a kind of managed chaos, with everything spic and span again when I woke each morning.

It wasn't long before Thys was onto me, wanting to know where I was and what I was doing. When I told him, he hit the roof. I said that I had no choice. The opportunity had come up, and I had grabbed it. That's not something the people in Basel understand. Thys said that he would call back, which meant that they would have a meeting about it. Which is what they do at the BIS.

I watched a lot of TV. The news was still full of doom and gloom, but the opinion of the talking heads had changed. It seemed like they had been reprogrammed. Someone important had decided that something had to be done to restore confidence, to stop the rot. Several big hitters on Wall Street, the few who hadn't been tainted by the financial collapse, were wheeled out to say how bullish they were. This was a once-in-a-lifetime buying opportunity. The viewer was reminded that investing is for the long term, and over the long term it has always worked out. I wondered what those big hitters were doing in private.

Out in the real world, things were getting worse by the day. A couple of the big car companies announced that they would go bust if they didn't get government help. It was a stupid thing to say, because a car company is different from most other companies. No one wants to buy a new car if there's a possibility of the manufacturer going belly-up, rendering the warranty worthless. And what were those cars going to be like, if they were built by employees who knew that they'd soon be out of a job? Would they really care to ensure that every rivet was in place?

But the management of these companies said that they were going bust, so the few sales they were making dried up completely. Those guys knew they wouldn't be allowed to fail because they were too big and important to the economy. So they put a gun against the government's head and said 'bail us out or else we're going under, and by the way, now that we said that publicly, we're *definitely* going under.' So the government had no choice but to bail them out. But at least they fired those managers in the process.

In an attempt to restore confidence in the banks, the government announced a series of 'stress tests'. These were a set of really bad theoretical scenarios that they would subject the banks to, running the numbers to see if they could still remain standing. Those that failed would be forced to raise more capital. Those that couldn't would be taken over.

In the two weeks that I waited, I never caught even a glimpse of Klein. He had the entire top floor of the mansion to himself. Nobody went upstairs unless summoned. Nobody, that is, except the children, who scampered up and down the main staircase with impunity. Klein had everything brought up to him, though from what I could tell he required very little.

Vance let it slip that there was a separate set of stairs at the back. It was a standard feature in those old houses, a concealed stairway for the servants to move unobtrusively about. Apparently Klein only ever came downstairs at night, and in the summer he would walk around the grounds while everyone was sleeping. Klein didn't smoke or drink. His only vice was chewing gum, and the only sign that he had been somewhere would be a chewed-up piece of gum stuck to a doorframe, or a wall, or a tree trunk.

By the second week I had serious cabin fever. The beautiful spring weather had continued for several days after I arrived, filling even the deepest recesses of the house with warm sunshine. But the second week was overcast and the place was very gloomy. I found myself turning on lights, only to find them switched off when I returned.

I was coming to the realisation that I'd never see Klein. I was caught in a game, everything in that house being a game of sorts. The world outside revolved around Klein, while in there, so close to the source, reality was suspended altogether.

Thys kept hounding me, demanding to know what was going on. I didn't bother trying to mollify him. I knew the tables had been turned, and I was now in charge. No matter how much Thys tried to assert his authority, in reality he had lost all leverage over me. He was just a two-bit actor like everyone else. Having said that he didn't want me to meet Klein on my own, he panicked when I lost my patience and said that I might as well walk away without any meeting at all.

I had given up believing that I would actually get to see Klein, but for as long as I was there, I had power. Maybe I would end up like Vance, staying forever, essentially lost but never forgotten. Not for as long as Klein held the outside world enthralled.

At first, whenever Thys called I would take care not to be overhead. After a while I didn't care, and would walk around the house speaking loudly into the phone and wondering if it echoed up those stairs. I was actually on the phone to him when Vance appeared at my side at the end of the second week. Something was different. I ended the call.

"You can go up," he said, and left the room.

I walked to the staircase. It felt surreal as I slowly ascended, as if I were a kid in a Jack in the Beanstalk production. But there was no giant waiting for me at the top. Well, none that I could see. It was really dark up there. A corridor extended the length of the house, all the doors along it closed. The window at the end let in some of the grey morning light, but that was all.

"Hello?" I called out.

I could hear footsteps downstairs, as if someone was running to see what it was.

I was about to call out again, when I heard a muffled voice. "In here."

I turned around. The door behind me was ajar. I walked up and pushed it open. There was no light in the room apart from a bank of eight screens atop a desk against the far wall. Klein had turned around in his chair and was facing me, silhouetted by the flickering numbers on the screens behind.

"Dr Klein?" I said. "I'm Chris Carraway."

He watched me for a few moments, and then the chair creaked as he stood up. Without saying anything, he walked into an adjoining room.

I followed him into a simple lounge, where some armchairs clustered around a coffee table. The window blind was closed, letting in just a sliver of light. Klein switched on a lamp in the corner, filling the room with its tungsten glow.

He picked up a jug from the table and poured himself a glass of water before sitting down in the nearest armchair.

He was easily recognisable from his photo in the BIS dossier. It was over ten years old, but he didn't look much different. He was pale in the photo, but seemed tanned next to the lamp. He was in his late sixties, but he looked lean and well exercised for someone who never went outside. For some reason I'd expected him to have a goatee like Vance's, but he was clean-shaven.

"How has your stay been?" said Klein, taking a sip of water.

"Fine, thank you."

He sat for a moment with the glass on his knee, watching me. "Your people are worried."

I nodded.

"Is that why they sent you?"

"Partly."

He looked towards the window. The blind was framed by sunlight from the window behind. "There's panic out there. The world is coming to an end. They must be wondering what their employee has been doing all this time."

"Waiting to see you," I said.

Klein turned to look at me. "Has it been worth the wait?"

"I don't know yet."

"They have a big problem. You're waiting around for a solution?"

"I'm not sure there is one."

"A problem without a solution." He smiled, slowly turning the glass in his hands. "So what exactly is this problem of yours?"

That put me on the spot. "Where do you want me to start?" I said.

"You mean you don't know?"

"Financial collapse, spreading like a forest fire without firebreaks, consuming everything-"

He shook his head. "Why resort to metaphors? Their problem is simply that the truth has been uncovered."

"What truth is that?" I asked.

"Nothing your people didn't already know. Something they always took for granted."

"Such as?"

Klein frowned, taking another sip of water. "What does your organisation do?"

"They aim to maintain financial stability. To ensure that the banking system-"

"*They*? Are you not a part of it?"

"To be honest, no. No, I'm not. In the sense that-"

"Your people are trying to protect their precious banks. No doubt you have a lot of analysts toiling away, calculating what's required to keep the banks safe. But for all those calculations, right now most of them stand to collapse. So what have you missed?"

"That's what I'm trying to find out."

"Something your spreadsheets cannot take into account. The business of banking is built on trust, nothing more. Banks take money from depositors, who believe the money will still be there when they come back for it. In turn, the banks lend that money to people who they believe will pay them back. If someone defaults, the whole chain comes down like a line of dominos. You want some water?" he said, pushing the jug towards me.

I shook my head.

"It's hardly surprising that the people who build financial models are frustrated. They would dearly love their spreadsheets to have the same exactitude, the same robustness as scientific models. Ditto for all those economists, consumed by envy of the sciences as they engage in their useless profession. All they're doing is tinkering with insights. They haven't achieved universal truths." Klein reached across to the window, parting the blinds with a finger. "Why are they content to remain dwarves, hankering after the shadows of giants?"

"Because they have nothing else?"

Klein nodded as he looked out the window. I could see a sliver of Long Island Sound, blindingly bright in that dark room. After several moments he let the blind fall back and turned to me. "They should chuck the whole thing and start afresh."

"And do what?" I said.

"You think I have the answer to that?"

"You have an opinion of what's wrong. Given your intellect, I'd imagine you have an idea of how to put it right."

Klein frowned as he looked at me. "Do *you* know what's wrong?"

"Not entirely," I said.

"They're basing everything on the principle of an equilibrium. But there is no such thing as equilibrium in a dynamic system. They don't seem to understand that instability is the natural way of things. Life by its very essence is dynamic. Equilibrium means death." Klein paused for a moment, looking into the glass of water in his hand. "You've heard of Brownian Motion?"

I nodded. "Somewhere back in high school physics. But the details escape me."

He frowned. "How could you forget?"

"It was some time ago."

Klein shook his head. "In the early nineteenth century, the Scottish botanist Robert Brown happened to be examining particles of pollen floating on a pond. They were inanimate particles, but on closer examination they were revealed to be somehow very much alive." Klein paused, looking at me. "What did people do with that observation?"

"As I remember, it confirmed the existence of atoms."

Klein shook his head. "I'm not talking about the source, I'm talking about the movement itself. What did people do with that? What could they possibly do with something so beautiful?"

"I don't know."

"They squeezed the life out of it."

I didn't know how to answer him. I was finding it increasingly difficult to keep up. "What do you mean?" I said after a few moments.

"The movement of each particle was random, but if you measured them over and over and over, a pattern emerged. A wonderfully complete, graceful pattern. A pattern that people seized on because it was confirmed in every measurement they made of the natural world. What did they call it?"

I shook my head.

"The Normal Distribution. Perhaps you have heard of it?"

I hate statistics. I know about the so-called Bell Curve, but couldn't say anything intelligent about it. They used to apply it to IQ tests at school, adjusting the results for the fact that most people are of average intelligence, with just a few being exceptionally bright and equally as few being exceptionally dumb. "Yes," I said, simply to hold Klein in conversation.

"Then you'll know that the Normal Distribution is used throughout the sciences as a simple model for complex phenomena. We humans love shoehorning everything to fit into its curve. Why do we do that? Why have we embraced it with such alacrity?"

I shrugged, shaking my head.

"Let me put it another way. What do people crave more than anything else?"

"Are you talking materially, psychologically, or spiritually-?"

"Don't dodge the question! What do people crave more than anything else?

"Wealth?" I said, knowing that it was a mistake.

"Don't make me throw you out of here."

I sat in uncomfortable silence, wondering what I could do to retrieve the conversation. I'd had my chance, but it was slipping through my fingers. A sensation I knew all too well.

Before I could think of anything to say, Klein put the glass down with a loud chink. "They crave certainty. People want a universal truth. They want something that is all-encompassing and explicable. People love the Normal Distribution, because it reduces life to normality."

Fortunately at that moment something started beeping in the adjoining room. Klein stood up and went to attend to whatever it was. He was gone for a few minutes while I sat in silence, trying to make sense of what he had been talking about.

I had got a bit here and there, but overall I was floundering. Thys hadn't wanted me to meet Klein. I thought he wanted to grab the limelight for himself, but in actual fact it was because I wasn't equipped to deal with Klein. I was way out of my depth. How did I ever think I could match up?

Klein re-entered the room and sat down.

"Well?" he said, looking at me.

"It makes sense."

"How so?"

"People crave certainty, and the Normal Distribution tells us that life is certain."

Klein nodded. "And how does it do that?"

I shrugged. "You'll have to tell me."

"By embracing the mean. When you are dealing with a very large number of observations, they cluster around an average, a mean. It sits at the apex of the bell curve. The further you move away from the mean, the odds of a deviation from that mean decline at an exponential rate.

The greater the population of observations, the more powerful the averaging effect. The heights of trees in a forest perfectly fit a bell curve, such that the height of a single tree isn't significant enough to alter the average of the whole forest.

So you don't have to worry about a particularly high tree, because the normal distribution tells you it won't exist. Just like a person with exceptional IQ. They probably won't exist. A category five hurricane will probably never hit New York."

I sat watching Klein for a few moments, regretting that I wasn't better prepared. Thys had told me to go off and do some research. I hadn't taken him seriously, just like I hadn't taken anything that I had ever done particularly seriously. But if there's anything I've learned, it's that you don't necessarily need ability. You just need to know what people want.

It was clear that Klein wanted to talk. He was sitting all alone up there, and he had something to say. As ill-equipped as I was to understand him, I was someone he could talk to. I was a neutral party, so to speak. And for some reason, I liked him. Maybe he knew that. So I sat in silence, as though I was digesting what he had said.

There wasn't a sound in the room. After what seemed like an age, Klein's chair creaked as he reached for his glass and took another sip of water. "Humans hate randomness. We want to know that there's a reason for everything. If a plane falls out of the sky onto your house, you want it to be explicable. Not that you were the victim of a freak event, with no ability to affect the outcome.

The way we have evolved is by learning from experience, and applying it to the future. That has served us well for the most part. Hence the Normal Distribution, which gives us the comfort that extreme events, events which lie more than five standard deviations from the average, are virtually impossible. Which is good enough for our miserably short lifespans." Klein smiled, examining the back of his hand while he held the glass, as if marvelling at the wrinkles of his own age.

"Evolution is just a numbers game. For ninety-nine point nine nine nine percent of the time humans have done rather well; they have continued in existence and taken control of the planet. Or so we believe. Of course, with that mindset we will be unable to cope with the one event that will make us extinct. It's virtually impossible, but not completely impossible." He let his hand drop and looked across at me. "Are you following me?"

"You're saying that we're currently experiencing one of those events?"

Klein laughed. "Not even close."

"You're saying that you're a part of it?"

He shook his head. "I'm saying that everyone is a part of it. *I* shouldn't be the one that your masters are so worried about. It should be everyone else. All those people attempting to mimic me, so that when I move, they all move too." Klein smiled. "Maybe that's it. You can go back to Basel and tell them you've found the reason for this crazy volatility in the market. Klein's algorithms have been uncovered and the thundering herd are charging after them. It's everyone else you've got to worry about, not me."

I shook my head. "I don't think that's the answer."

"Why not?"

"Because you would have moved on. It makes no sense to have everyone following behind."

"It does if I'm ahead of them, be it by seconds or even milliseconds. Ahead is ahead. I let them follow. I lead, and they follow. A perfect arrangement, if there ever was one."

"Is that the arrangement, as you call it?"

Klein smiled again. "Why on earth would I tell you?"

"You're saying that you're the cause? Everything is correlated with what you're doing?"

He laughed, shaking his head. "I'm far humbler than that. No, the cause is the very thing that the whole world has been rushing headlong towards for decades now." He sat watching me while I wondered what that could be.

Mercifully, Klein didn't expect an answer. "I'm talking globalisation," he said after a few moments. "We've been told that it makes the world richer, and it has. For once, a grand scheme seems to have worked. But everything has a price. Because it is an uncomfortable truth, no one has been prepared to consider it."

Without waiting for a response, he continued. "Globalisation creates the appearance of stability, but by interlocking everything with everything else, you end up with huge instability. Everything is interconnected and interrelated. As you said when you walked in here, it's a forest without firebreaks." He paused, looking out the window. "That is the cause of all this correlation, not me."

Once again, I don't think Klein expected a reply. We had settled into a kind of relationship where he talked and I listened, without any pretence that I understood everything that he was talking about.

We sat in silence for a few moments, and then he let the blind drop and turned back to the room. "Financial theory defines risk as the extent to which prices vary around their mean. Observing how they have moved in relation to each other in the past allows a precise and measurable trade-off between risk and return. It assumes the correlations of the past will be the correlations of the future." Klein smiled, shaking his head.

"It's like saying that someone's character doesn't change. For most of the time, it doesn't. The Normal Distribution holds. But if you've inhabited the real world, you'll know that at times of high stress, people change. Someone you thought you knew well can behave like a complete stranger when subjected to extreme stress.

It's the same with markets, because they are nothing more than a collection of people, all bidding against each other. The central assumption of the Efficient Markets Theory is that investors behave rationally at all times, but of course they don't. Any fool knows that."

I looked up as there was a knock at the door, but Klein didn't seem to notice.

"Humans crave certainty, but real world events are not well-behaved, or certain. And when it comes to the market, things are even worse. Humans are prone to bouts of excessive optimism or pessimism. That throws an already unruly system way off any course plotted by a Normal Distribution."

There was another knock at the door.

"Yes?" said Klein.

The door opened and Vance looked into the room. "Danilo's here."

"So?"

"He wants to speak with you."

"Tell him to wait."

"He says it's urgent."

"Tell him to wait."

Vance hesitated for a moment, then disappeared from the door.

I realised that my audience with Klein might be over, yet I hadn't got onto anything that mattered. No hard numbers, for a start.

"Can I ask a question?" I said, sitting forward in the chair.

Klein nodded.

"When I was trying to track you down, I got the message over and over again that the Atracor funds are closed. That there's no way anyone can get in. But when I posed as an investor, suddenly those private bankers came running back to me, saying they could get me in. They both had the same story that it was exclusive to him, and him alone."

Klein shrugged. "Have you never sold anything?"

"You're saying it's a marketing strategy?"

"These people are salesmen. What do you expect?"

"But why do they feel the need to do that? Your track record sells itself."

Klein smiled. "Have you ever worked in this industry?"

I shook my head.

"It's the most measurable industry in the world. Performance of every fund is perfectly quantifiable, at any point in time. So an investor should have a purely objective decision to make. Right?"

I nodded. "That's what I was getting at."

"Well you would be wrong. It's not about objectivity, but perception. It's no different from the markets, where you are dealing with the collective psychology of millions of people. Perception *is* reality."

I looked up as the door swung open. A thickset man stood there, arms folded. "What's going on?" he said.

"Why aren't you in Manhattan?" said Klein.

"What the hell is going on? What is this guy doing here? What are you telling him?"

Klein shrugged. "What he needs to know."

The man's face stiffened. "I want a word, now."

Klein turned to me and smiled. "Allow me to introduce my second-in-command, Danilo di Pasquantonio."

The man didn't look at me. He was really angry, but Klein didn't show the slightest concern. He glanced at Di Pasquantonio. "Join our discussion, if you want."

The man looked at me with dangerous eyes. "What the fuck do you want?"

"I'm interviewing Dr Klein. I'm-"

"The fuck you are. You think we bought that crap about you being an investor?" He turned to Klein. "He posed as an investor, and pitched up at our London office."

Klein nodded. "I heard about that."

"Yeah," said Di Pasquantonio. "They saw through it in London. But not in New York, I'm sorry to say. Right under my nose. I'll find out who's responsible."

"It was me," said Klein.

There was a look on Di Pasquantonio's face which I'm sure nobody had ever seen before. He recovered quickly and turned back to me. "Get out of here," he said.

I shook my head. "I didn't make any false claims in New York. I just said that I wanted to meet with Dr Klein."

"What for?"

"I'm with the Bank for International Settlements."

"You think that gives you the right to walk in here? Nobody, but nobody gets to see Dr Klein. Certainly not some fuckhead from Switzerland."

I looked to Klein to see what he would say, but he was watching Di Pasquantonio, a slightly amused smile on his face.

"I'm not going to ask you again. Get out of here!"

I stood up and walked out the door. He didn't move aside, so I had to slip around him, in dangerous proximity to a man who looked like he wanted to break my neck.

Vance was standing right outside. He avoided my gaze and I walked downstairs, not sure whether I should be leaving altogether.

As I reached the bottom of the stairs, I heard footsteps behind me. It was Vance.

"Just wait a bit," he said softly. "Wait here until they're finished."

I nodded, walking towards the sofa that I had been occupying for most of the past two weeks.

"Not there," said Vance, glancing at the stairs. "Don't let Danilo see you when he leaves."

12

"I didn't hear from Klein again that day. I was helping myself to some lunch in the kitchen when I got a call from Thys, wanting to know what was going on. I don't think he believed me when I told him that I'd met Klein, especially when I was unable to answer any questions. Just what had we talked about? Certainly nothing that Basel would be interested in.

Should I have told him that I wasn't able to understand much of what Klein had said? Or that he was off the wall and barely intelligible? Or that he was lonely and bored, and while he dabbled with the markets he needed something closer at hand to play with? Someone who would run off to his masters with a tale of gobbledygook? After all, Klein was a master at sowing confusion in the markets.

Instead, I made up something about Klein agreeing to 'a framework of discussion', or something like that. Something

Basel would understand. And of course Thys liked it. He said he would email a list of questions he wanted answered. He said he would come over personally to attend. Perhaps some other people from Basel too, and some from New York.

No, I said. Absolutely not. Klein was adamant that he would speak to me alone. Why? Thys wanted to know. Klein trusted me, was my reply. Klein liked me and trusted me.

Did I tell him that I wasn't in Klein's league? That I quite simply wasn't equipped to deal with the man one-on-one? Of course not. Klein was the best thing going for me. For once in my life, I had something that everyone else wanted, and I would keep it all to myself. Whether or not I was deserving, or equipped to deal with it wasn't the issue. Who really deserves anything they get in life?

Then came the really important question: When was my next meeting with Klein? I smiled. How should I know? I wasn't even sure if he would see me again. I stumbled so badly in our first meeting that he probably would have thrown me out that very morning, had Di Pasquantonio not intervened. I was saved by the man who wanted me out of there that instant.

But the people in Basel would never know that. All they'd ever hear was what I told them. As much as it irritated Thys, the reality was that he was completely beholden to me. I didn't bother opening the attachment when he emailed his list of questions. I knew that Klein would tell me only what he wanted to, and nothing more.

So I did what I had become good at doing, which was to wait for something to happen. Another week went by, and then another. The results of the bank stress tests were published, and of course there were no amazing revelations.

It was just as everyone had expected, which was the

whole point of the exercise. Essentially it was an artifice. The authorities knew which banks were considered tainted by the market, and which were okay. So they had to fail the former, and pass the latter. It was essentially a double-bluff which everyone involved knew and accepted.

The market needed the confidence that the banks were okay, or if they weren't okay it needed to have a line drawn under that, a specific figure for how much they weren't okay. Those banks were then forced to raise the money, and then the whole show could go on. For once, the market accepted what the authorities said. The market knew full well that it was a bluff, but without it, nothing could continue. Confidence would once again evaporate, and the whole system would collapse.

Some of the banks even went so far as to pre-announce their upcoming earnings, reporting that they were profitable once more. That was nonsense, because large banks have so much leeway to revalue their assets and liabilities. A lot of the instruments they use aren't traded openly, so the price is whatever they want it to be. That means they can report pretty much any figure they like over the short term.

But it worked. It was meaningless and you could say desperate, but it lifted the markets and commentators in the media were gushing about a 'return to normality' and 'pulling back from the brink'. Taking their cue, economists started talking about 'green shoots' when they were apoplectic just a few months previously.

Those same economists hadn't predicted the financial collapse or the recession that followed. If you're in the prediction business and want to keep your job, you should always follow a simple rule: Never be wrong on your own. It's fine to be wrong along with everyone else, but if you're wrong on your own, you're toast.

So it was hardly surprising that none of those economists had been brave enough to take a knife to their forecasts and slash them, even when it was clear to just about everyone that the world was in serious trouble.

Instead, they'd slowly edged their numbers down, all the time watching to see what their peers were doing. And in doing so they had all followed the economy like lemmings off a cliff, just as the banks had followed the property bubble right up to the point where it burst in their faces.

But those same economists were now starting to edge their numbers up, so everything was okay again. And the sun was shining. It was mid May, and it felt like summer. For the first time since arriving there, I took a walk outside. No one stopped me.

I wandered down to the water, and stood on the dock. The boathouse was right alongside, the door standing open to reveal a seductive sliver of white. I stepped inside. It was a Ferretti, a beautiful Italian motorboat about twenty metres long. She sat absolutely still in the water, her chrome fittings polished to a high sheen. Like the boats in Monaco, she looked too perfect to have ever been used.

Something made me climb into the cockpit. There was a key in the ignition and I turned it a notch. The fuel gauge didn't move. Klein wasn't going anywhere anytime soon. I walked back to the house, to find Vance waiting for me on the lawn outside. Klein wanted to see me.

I couldn't walk in again totally unprepared, to be told things that could well have been invaluable, but were lost on me. But what had I done since I had last seen Klein? Nothing at all. I had thought about what he had said endlessly, but it was kind of like looking at a master painting. Knowing that it was great, without really understanding why. At heart, my real problem was that I had no idea what I wanted to get out of it. Certainly nothing that Basel wanted.

I didn't have time to come up with a game plan, so I simply went inside and ascended the stairs. The door to Klein's office was ajar as before, and I walked across the landing and pushed it open without announcing myself.

Klein was at his desk, studying the screens in front of him.

"Dr Klein?" I said.

He didn't reply at first, moving the mouse to click on interconnected windows full of flickering numbers.

"What have you been waiting around for?" he said without looking away from his screens.

"To see you," I said.

"We've already had our meeting."

"It was interrupted."

"For good reason."

I stood there for a few moments, not knowing what to say. "I want to find out the truth," I said at last.

Klein's hand paused on the mouse.

"As you said, everyone has an opinion of you. I want to find the truth."

Klein didn't reply. I decided to up the ante. "They say that you're inhuman. An ogre, eating away at the common man. Feasting on all his hard-earned money."

Klein released the mouse. His chair squeaked as he swivelled around, a faint smile on his lips. "The most suspicious minds are those of the guilty. Have you heard of Keynes?"

I nodded. "John Maynard Keynes, the great British economist."

"Good that you remember something. Keynes wrote an essay in the nineteen thirties, right in the middle of the Great Depression. He was optimistic. He noted the world's steadily rising per capita wealth over the centuries. He extrapolated it over the next hundred years, predicting that

Western society would achieve such a level of wealth that it would no longer concern itself with money. Everyone's basic needs would be addressed, such that we could be released from acquisitiveness to appreciate life and learn to live it to the full."

Klein turned back to his screens, taking hold of the mouse again as he watched the columns of numbers flickering in front of him. "We're almost at that point, one hundred years on. The great economist was wrong. He was right about the wealth that we would achieve, but wrong about what we would do with it. The human race is more acquisitive than ever."

I watched the cursor drifting across Klein's screens as he moved his mouse, closing windows, opening new ones. All filled with columns of numbers.

"Do you know how much money is made each year on Wall Street?" he said after a few moments.

"Several billion?" I said.

"*Several*?" Klein laughed. "Hundreds of billions. Hundreds of billions, and yet the financial industry is a zero sum game. Net-net, it adds nothing to the economy. It produces nothing. No cars, no cans of baked beans. It doesn't wait on tables, it doesn't fly us anywhere, and it doesn't rake the leaves from our lawns.

It's a giant tick, riding on the back of the economy and sucking blood out of it. Why does that happen? How do those bankers get to keep so much of the money that they skim off everyone else?"

I shrugged. "Most people aren't good with numbers. They can't work out which is the best mortgage, or even what their monthly budget should be."

"Give people more credit than that. The answer is the banks have become too powerful. This country is no different from a banana republic, hijacked by the ruling elite and run in their interests. The banks have lobbied for more and more deregulation, which has allowed them to do as they please." I saw Klein smile as he watched his screens. "They've got what they deserve."

Something beeped on his desk.

"Do you want to get that?" I said, because I couldn't think of anything else to say.

He waved his hand dismissively. "You think I'm a slave to my Bloomberg terminal? Chained to it twenty-four hours a day?"

I shook my head.

"The system runs itself. I designed it to be very responsive and very flexible. It's well near perfect. But if you listened to anything that I said before, you'll know that chasing perfection is like chasing the horizon. You'll never get there. So I keep an eye on it, waiting for the moment it fails."

"So the famous Klein algorithms aren't infallible."

Klein released the mouse and swivelled around to face me again, frowning. "Who says otherwise?"

"Just about everyone I've spoken to."

"What would they know? How can an algorithm possibly be infallible?"

"Your track record would say so."

He smiled, his face lit blue as he turned back to the screens on his desk. "This is not a science. It's anything but a science. It's art, but art without the emotion. Can you understand that? Most people can't."

"Maybe that's why you're such a mystery."

Klein didn't reply as he typed on the keyboard. I waited a few moments, hoping that he would say something. He didn't.

I upped the ante once more. "A mystery that's misunderstood can very easily become a monster."

Klein stopped typing and turned to face me. "Why? I understand the human condition better than anyone." He tapped his finger on one of the screens. "After all, what are these markets, other than the interconnected emotions of millions of people? Do you know what they tell you?"

I shook my head.

"They tell you that human nature never changes. That means there will always be asset bubbles, and there will always be financial crises. No matter how much people think they've learned from the last one, the last two, the last ten. Nothing inspires people to act quite so stupidly as the fear of missing out. Just look how they behave around a buffet table, or at a one-day sale.

A financial bubble like we've just experienced has nothing to do with evil individuals manipulating the market to the detriment of everyone else. Yet the politicians are blaming short-sellers and speculators for the current mess. But these very people are critical to the functioning of markets. Without them, prices wouldn't clear. For every buyer, you need a seller, and vice-versa. When markets were soaring, you didn't hear a squeak from politicians that short-sellers were getting fried."

Klein had become quite animated. I got a sense that I was witnessing a side to him that had rarely been seen before. I waited in silence for him to continue.

"But their knee-jerk reaction right now is to appease the baying mob. Will those politicians do anything to address the real problem? Of course not. At best they won't challenge the system at all, but let it continue to grow unfettered because that's where their tax dollars come from. At worst, they'll pursue a short-term result, rather than acting in our long term interest. They'll rush to save a popping bubble by inflating another." Klein paused, taking a sip of water from the glass on his desk. "You know what Einstein said about infinity?"

I shook my head.

"He said that both the universe and human stupidity are infinite. But he was more certain about the latter."

I smiled. Klein did not.

"Because of human greed and human fear, bubbles are forever. I observe, and I take note. Does that make me a bad man? Just because those people getting fried cannot separate their emotions from reality?"

Without waiting for a reply, he continued. "The cornerstone of modern financial theory presumes that everyone behaves rationally at all times. Yet that is untrue. The financial industry has been built on it, and it's not true." Klein waved his hand across the screens in front of him. "The Efficient Markets Hypothesis presumes that every price is an accurate indicator of a stock's intrinsic value. Yet we've seen some of these prices falling ninety percent and shooting up five hundred percent. How can that be 'efficient'?

If these prices reflect all available information, why would anyone trouble to obtain it? Why would they trade between themselves, taking different views of the same future? There would be no point to it at all."

He paused, taking another sip of water. "It is not me who your masters should be worrying about. I am merely the person who has spotted the flaw. They still cling to it, like blind men."

I nodded. "I guess they do."

"Then why do you work for them?"

All I could think of saying was "I don't, really."

Klein frowned. "So what do you do?"

"I'm finding my way. I grabbed this opportunity, because I thought it might help me find my way."

Klein looked at me for a few moments. "What are you going to tell them?"

"That's the hard part. Everything we've been talking about isn't what they want to hear. They want facts, they want figures."

Klein smiled. "What did I tell you before? Everyone wants certainty. The lesser the man, the more he craves it."

Klein turned back to his screens, as though they were an audience. He sat watching them for a few moments, and said something I didn't catch.

"What was that?" I said.

He turned back to me. "You can't blame them. They've been conditioned to it. You can't tell people that the pensions for which they've worked forty years rely on mere suppositions. That the economy which employs them is based on nothing more than animal instincts. They want to hear that it's all controllable and predictable. That it's a science that can be exactly measured and for which the final outcome is known and quantified and could never be otherwise.

But that's not the truth. The truth is shocking. Their pensions are dependent on whims and fancies, impulses and passions. Everything they have saved all their working lives could be worth everything, and nothing. There is no certainty. Life hangs on a thread."

Something beeped again and he sat forward in his chair and began typing on the keyboard.

The conversation was going better than the previous one. At least I didn't feel like a complete idiot. I was achieving something, without really knowing what it was.

But I knew if I could just get a few figures out of Klein, I would have struck gold. If I could quantify how big his fund was, I would know something that everyone else wanted.

I watched him typing for a bit longer, running my tongue across my teeth. "To be honest, Basel's main problem is not knowing. They have no idea what your overall exposure is. If you could just give me a few hard numbers-"

Klein sighed as he continued typing. "You want to know the biggest problem of all? There's too much information. People are building bigger and bigger databases, hoovering up more and more of it. But more information doesn't equate to more knowledge. In fact, quite the opposite.

Most of it is at best useless. At worse, it actually degrades knowledge. In their search for exactitude, for certainty, people achieve ignorance." He finished typing and sat back in his chair. "Every single financial model being used out there attempts to predict the future by looking at the past. What do they say about hindsight? It's twenty-twenty. That twenty-twenty vision blinds you to the truth."

I stood watching him, not having moved from the doorway. I would have sat down, but there was no other chair in the room. I felt that Klein wanted to tell me something. I just had to push carefully ahead, and he would tell me. I coughed, clearing my throat. "What scares Basel is the sheer scale of your operation, the influence you have on markets around the world."

Klein didn't reply, watching his screens.

"If you could quantify that, it would take some of the heat off you because their biggest bugbear is not knowing."

Klein turned around. He was smiling. "The heat isn't on me at all. It's on them. They're the ones who are worried."

"You're saying they shouldn't be?"

Klein shook his head. "They should be terrified."

"Of what you could do?"

"As I said before, it's not me they should be worried about. It's the herd following behind. That herd of supposedly rational people. Cows walk willingly into the slaughterhouse. They don't need to be dragged."

"That's not a good analogy. We've made them that way."

"And haven't we made ourselves that way, too?"

"You're talking about investors?"

He shook his head. "I'm talking about the human race. Our entire history of evolution, our very makeup, contains one critical flaw. We haven't encountered something that is more than ten standard deviations from the mean of human evolutionary experience." Klein looked up at me. "Do you know what I mean by ten standard deviations?"

I shook my head. He was back to the Normal Distribution, which meant that he had lost me once more.

"To save myself from getting tongue-tied, a mere five standard deviations, or five sigma, comprises ninety-nine point nine nine nine nine percent of total outcomes. You will then appreciate that something beyond ten standard deviations is an event that the human brain would have never encountered."

"You think it will happen?"

"Of course," he nodded. "I have demonstrated in my models that it will happen. And by embracing that, I am saving humanity from itself. Saving it from that flaw, that blind-spot which could well destroy it."

He smiled, shaking his head. "I'm getting carried away. Not a case of complete destruction, but certainly something that would knock us off the perch of so-called civilisation which we have achieved. And that will feel very, very uncomfortable for everyone. Maybe not for the lowliest rice farmer, but certainly for everyone else.

"You're saying that things will get worse from here?"

Klein smiled again. "Unimaginable, isn't it? Certainly something that no one would want to consider. But that doesn't mean it won't happen. We humans have a tendency to confuse what we would like to happen with what will actually happen."

"You're saying that you can bring about that event?"

"I'm saying that I know something that no one else does. I'm watching something that no one else is watching."

"Which is?"

"I've already told you.""

Carraway stopped as Valassis stood up.

"Where the hell have you been?" he shouted.

Two Vietnamese men were approaching the boat. One of them was supporting the other.

"Jesus! Have you been drinking?"

They didn't reply, stopping at the edge of the quay.

"You've been fucking drinking again. I told you, no drinking on this boat. You want to do that, you stay behind. I get someone else." He turned around. "Lan!" he called out.

She appeared in the doorway. She must have been waiting just inside the cabin.

"You tell them to get their shit together, or they're off this boat. Tell them that. And tell them to make ready. We're leaving now. And I mean right now."

Lan said something to the men in Vietnamese. Without replying, they stepped aboard and headed along the deck to the bow.

Valassis turned around to face Carraway. "It's time you cut to the chase."

Carraway looked up at him. "I'm almost there."

"You've been saying that for the last hour. Time to come clean. Just what is it about Klein that you want to say?"

Carraway smiled. "Maybe you could tell me first what your interest in him is."

"It doesn't work like that. You're a guest on my boat."

He shrugged. "I can easily get off."

"Fuck you. What is it about Klein that you want to say?"

"Tell me first what he is to you."

"So you can change your story?"

"My story won't change, I promise. And I'm near the end. Really, I am"

Valassis shook his head. "You'll end it right now by telling us what you found."

"If he's close to the end, let him finish the story," I said.

Valassis ignored me, his eyes fixed on Carraway. "I want to know what you found. I want to know what you spent all that time looking for."

"Let him finish the story," said Jongstra.

"It's only a story if he found something." Valassis steadied himself as the boat rocked in the wake of a passing barge. "What did you find?" he said, standing over Carraway.

"I found nothing."

"So you have no story."

"My story is that at the end of it, I found nothing."

"So you wasted everyone's time, ours included." Valassis turned to the cabin door. "Lan!" he called out. "Tell them to cast off! We're leaving."

There was no reply from down below. Valassis turned back to us, pointedly ignoring Carraway. "Gentlemen, I need to cast off. No moorings here tonight."

We stood up, thanking him for his hospitality. I disembarked, followed by Jongstra, with Carraway behind him.

The three of us stood on the quayside, watching as the two crewmen began untying the hawsers. Valassis got behind the wheel and started the engine. The street hawkers who had been watching us earlier reappeared out of the crowd. They stood silently to the side, their baskets slung over their shoulders.

"You didn't tell us what Klein is to you," called out Carraway.

Valassis didn't reply, watching his crew pull the fenders aboard. After a few moments he turned to look at us. "How do you think I got all this?" he said.

None of us replied.

"I own a chain of car dealerships. A mid-sized chain. I built it from nothing, and it's done pretty well for me. But that wouldn't be enough to get me this. Not at fifty-five. Not unless I wanted to work for another ten years." Valassis turned the wheel and the yacht's bow swung away from the quayside, pulling the forward hawser tight.

"I made money, but more importantly I made it work for me. Klein provided all of this. Because of Klein I can retire early, I can have all this. That's what Klein is to me." Valassis checked his crew's progress. They had released all the hawsers except for the one at the bow. The yacht was ready to go, its nose pointing out into the river, pulling tight against the remaining hawser while the brown river water churned white behind its stern.

Valassis looked back at Carraway. "Then you come with some cockeyed story that there's something untoward, something hidden. You make me sit and listen like an idiot when you just wanted to string me along. You want to know about Klein? I've never even met the man, but I can tell you he's a genius, pure and simple."

"You're sure about that?" said Carraway.

"You'll never recognise ability in anyone if you've never amounted to anything. Of course he's a genius. He has to be a genius, there's no way he can't be. All my money is with him. All my clients' money is with him. All my family's money, and all my friends too. All of it's with

Klein because I know that he's for real. I know he's the real deal."

Valassis whistled and one of the crewmen released the remaining hawser. He gunned the engine and his yacht slipped away, pushing between the sampans.

We stood on the quayside along with our attendant street hawkers, watching the yacht heading out across the river. The sun was low and the brown water shone like gold.

13

"Is that what happened?" said Jongstra.

Carraway didn't reply as he watched the yacht motoring away, its wake criss-crossed by sampans.

"Is that really what happened? You found nothing?"

Carraway smiled. "You don't want to have wasted your time?"

Jongstra shook his head. "I don't think that's what happened. I think it was something else."

Carraway looked back at the yacht. "In a way, it was true. And Valassis wanted to go. He's got to be out of the delta by nightfall." Carraway smiled again. "Judging by the flow of the river, I'd say that he's heading in the wrong direction. Going upstream, instead of out to sea."

Several street hawkers had joined the others, and they stood in a circle around us, their shadows overlapping our own. We didn't make eye contact, and they didn't approach us. A stand-off at the calmest moment of the day, when the sunlight renders everything monumental with its shadows.

"How about finishing the story?" I said. "After all, we don't have to be anywhere."

Carraway turned away from the river. "As much as I tried to get some hard numbers from Klein, I got nowhere. It rapidly became clear that he had told me all he wanted to. I tried stalling, but I knew he was about to call the meeting to an end, and that I wouldn't be able to see him again.

He had communicated a message to me that I had somehow missed. He wasn't going to waste any more time with me. But how badly did he want that message relayed?

I had learned something from all those other meetings on my journey to find him. Pre-emptively I stood up, thanking him for his time.

"You'd like a taxi?" said Klein.

"Yes, thank you."

"You have what you wanted?"

"To take back to Basel?" I shook my head. "No, I don't."

He sat watching me, silhouetted by his screens. I was hoping that he would say something, but he didn't.

After a few moments, I cleared my throat. "I didn't expect to get anything. Not for them."

"And you? What did you want?"

"Something that no one else has."

He smiled. "You have that now?"

I shook my head.

"And you'll still go." Klein turned away, narrowing his eyes as he studied his screens.

I shrugged. "I guess that's the way it has to be."

"Has it been a waste of time?"

"No, I wouldn't say so."

He turned back to me. "So you have gained something."

"I think you're going to tell me."

Klein watched me for a few moments, and then reached for the glass and took a sip of water. "What does everyone say about me?"

"That you're ahead of the game. You lead, and everyone else follows. You make markets."

Klein nodded, looking into the glass. "I make markets. I am the market. I am the market, and you know what? I am nothing. Nothing at all."

"What do you mean?" I said.

He leaned back in his chair, crossing one leg over the other. "What did the people from Atracor tell you?"

I shrugged. "Nothing much. Nothing much at all."

"Think about it. What did they tell you?"

"That you don't see visitors, you're unreachable, you're not available."

Klein shook his head. "No, they said it wasn't about the money. Didn't they?"

"I guess so."

"They said it wasn't about the money, and they never knew just how true it was. There's no money at all."

"What?" I stared at him.

"There's nothing. I haven't made a trade for years."

"It's your algorithms, right? Your algorithms do everything, while you just watch."

He shook his head. "There's nothing here. Do you understand me? *Nothing*. There's some cash sitting in Atracor's corporate accounts. But after deducting our fees, and paying out the latest redemptions, there's not a hell of a lot left. Certainly none of those fabled billions which I supposedly control."

I stared at him. He watched me with a smile on his lips.

"But you move the markets."

"I don't. My reputation does."

"It's more than that. It has to be more than that."

"Remember what I said? Perception is reality."

"But I don't understand. Just how-?"

"When I started, I was the best and everyone noticed. I had very little in the way of assets. I wasn't interested in how much I managed. I wouldn't take any money from my friends, and that was when I still had some.

As my performance knocked the socks off everyone else, money came flooding in. It came from all quarters. People I had never seen or heard of would send me a wire transfer with an accompanying fax. Absolute trust, or total greed. You decide.

I was the best, but I was also lucky to get started when I did. My algorithms were designed to spot those rare, unexpected moves in the markets which by their very definition don't come round very often.

After an amazing beginning, when I alone made money while everyone else was losing, normality returned and my losing streak set in. It would be a long and painful one. Money had meant nothing to me when I started, but now it was everything. I could not let go.

I knew that my algorithms would ultimately triumph, but as much as anyone will tell you that investing is for the long term, no one sticks around if you're not performing in the short term.

No problem. I could pad things for now, to survive the drought. I started small at first, making fictitious trades, tinkering with the model in the hope that it would return to profit sooner than it should.

After a while it became all too easy. It generated its own momentum. As long as inflows were greater than outflows, the scam could continue. And inflows will always be greater than outflows, because success begets success. Even if that success isn't real. In fact, people want something that's too good to be true. They want to be blinded to the truth. As Goebbels said, the bigger the lie, the more people will believe.

Everyone accepted on blind faith anything that I said, and that power is very seductive. I knew I could do just about anything, and nobody would question it. Where else can you get power like that?" Klein smiled, sitting with his hands in his lap. "And the ultimate power is that I can bring it all down."

I stood watching him, wondering if he was playing with me. "What about your clients?" I said after a few moments. "Don't they mean anything to you?"

He laughed. "What's that saying? 'You can't cheat an honest man'. They've been dishonest by investing with me. If they put their greed aside for just a moment, they could plainly see that my means of generating those returns is dishonest. But they've chosen to accept it, embracing it for all that it can bring them. Dishonesty gets its reward."

"They've lost everything?"

He smiled. "It depends how you look at it. They may have gained something, without knowing it. But in terms of what they originally set out for, yes. They have lost everything. Everything, and more."

"How much is involved?"

He smiled again, shaking his finger at me. "In spite of yourself, you still want to take a number back to Basel. Let's just say there's one hell of a lot of money that quite simply doesn't exist. I wouldn't even know how much. Hundreds of billions would be a safe approximation. And then you have all those other billions that are trying to mimic me, copying a strategy that's completely fake."

"But if it's fake, it wouldn't work. And if it doesn't work, then nobody would have profited from following you."

Klein shook his head. "The shear weight of money creates a trend in itself. Just like any bubble, that carries it forward, creating its own returns."

"Not anymore it isn't. The market's down over thirty percent this year alone."

He winked at me. "Wait till you see how much it's down when news of this gets out."

"A fall more than ten standard deviations from the mean?"

Klein smiled. "So you have understood something after all." He paused, watching me. "I am giving you that event. That ten sigma event. An event so huge and unexpected, that it could very well bring down the economy on which the modern world is built. I have given it to you. Do with it what you will."

"Does anyone at Atracor know this?"

Klein shook his head.

"You've done it all on your own, without anyone knowing?"

He nodded.

"Just how is that possible?"

"Haven't you listened to what everyone has been telling you? I am Atracor. Atracor is me. Everyone else does as I say."

"Even di Pasquantonio?"

"Even him. He is an excellent watch dog. Disciplined, faithful, vicious. But a good watch dog guards the house. It is never let into the house." Klein glanced at his watch. "Time for you to go. Wait downstairs. A taxi will come for you."

Carraway stopped, watching the river. The incoming tide had eased and the water appeared still, held there by two opposing forces. When the tide began to ebb, the flow of the river would once more prevail, continuing its four thousand kilometre path to the sea.

"What did you do?" said Jongstra.

Carraway turned to look at him. "I went back to Basel, and gave them my report."

"What did it say?"

"Exactly what they wanted to hear."

"Which was not what you found, right?"

Carraway nodded. "Like I said, I gave them what they wanted. Everyone there likes a quiet life. Otherwise they'd be earning far more, working for an investment bank."

"You didn't tell them the truth?"

Carraway shook his head. "If I told the truth, it could bring about Klein's ten standard deviation event. An unimaginable hit to the global financial system."

"But why did he tell you?"

"He had made a mockery of the system, and he wanted it known. He had mocked the best and the brightest that this generation has produced."

"So what are you doing here?" I said. "Why didn't you report it?"

Carraway looked at me. "Would *you* report it?"

"That's not my job."

"And neither is it mine."

"Then why have you told us?"

"You wanted a story, I gave you one. As bored as he is, Valassis in particular wanted a story. It would have been a good one for him to hear, but he didn't want to wait for the end." Carraway smiled at each of us in turn. "Well, it was nice meeting you." He walked back along the quay.

"What are you going to do now?" I said.

"Grow rice," he said over his shoulder.

"Rice?"

He stopped, looking out at the opposite bank. "The Mekong delta has one of the highest yielding farmlands in the world. They get four harvests a year. And land is cheap since the currency devalued. That's why we're all here, right? Because we have a bit of money and everything's cheap. I don't know for how much longer that money's going to be around, but I do know that everyone will always need rice."

Carraway turned and looked down the river, but the yacht was lost amongst the boats and sampans. "As Valassis said, I'll never amount to anything. And he's right. After all, he's a man who can spot an opportunity, and he sees nothing in me.

But I can still amount to something, by not being much at all. No more than a rice farmer." He smiled at me. "I'm not going to be Klein's messenger. How about you?"

Made in the USA
Lexington, KY
16 June 2014